Mission: Cute French boyfriend . . .

I darted a quick glance at Alex. His large hands and long fingers practically swallowed the clay as he shaped and molded it. His face was set in absolute concentration. I imagined those hands caressing my cheek, massaging my neck and shoulders—*whoa!*

Where did that thought come from?

The last thing I wanted was for someone from Mustang, Texas, to fulfill my fantasies for a romantic year in Paris. And I absolutely did not want Alex Turner running his hands amok over my back. No. I wanted someone else. A French guy.

As discreetly as I could because I didn't want Alex to know what I was up to, I studied the guys in the class. Blonds, brunets, even a redhead. They all looked pretty serious about their project. That got them an extra point. Since art was my life, I wanted a guy who could relate, someone I could talk to about artistic endeavors.

There were a couple of really hot guys. They were much cuter than dull Alex Turner from Mustang. With his hair the color of mud and his soulful, brown eyes.

Tomorrow I would definitely have to get to class early so I could have the opportunity to sit by a Frenchie!

Year Abroad Trilogy

Paris: Alex & Dana

RACHEL HAWTHORNE

BANTAM BOOKS
NEW YORK · TORONTO · LONDON · SYDNEY · AUCKLAND

RL: 6, AGES 012 AND UP

PARIS: ALEX & DANA
A Bantam Book / October 2000

Cover photography by Michael Segal.

Produced by 17th Street Productions,
an Alloy Online, Inc. company.
33 West 17th Street
New York, NY 10011.

ISBN: 0-553-49327-2

Visit us on the Web! www.randomhouse.com/teens

Published simultaneously in the United States and Canada

Bantam Books is an imprint of Random House Children's Books, a
division of Random House, Inc. BANTAM BOOKS and the rooster
colophon are registered trademarks of Random House, Inc. Bantam Books,
1540 Broadway, New York, New York 10036.

PRINTED IN THE UNITED STATES OF AMERICA

OPM   0 9 8 7 6 5 4 3 2 1

For my mom, with love

Paris:
Alex &
Dana

One

Dana

I WAS AFRAID. Shaking in my boots afraid. The reality had finally hit home. Or I should say, it had hit Paris.

Paris, France! City of Light. City of romance. City of my dreams.

I hadn't realized until this moment as I stared out the window of my new bedroom how terrified I would be. Or how alone.

I, Dana Madison, born and raised in tiny Mustang, Texas, had never ventured beyond the Texas border, and here I was, thousands of miles from said border. It was beyond comprehension. Terribly exciting! And incredibly frightening.

I had been looking forward to this moment for so long that I was having a difficult time reconciling the terror gripping me. With a lot of cajoling, pleading, and promises never to ask for anything else as long as I lived, I'd managed to convince my parents to let me take part in the Year Abroad program. Paris had been my city of choice—for its art, but more important, for its romantic guys.

For a whole year I would go to a school in Paris—starting tomorrow. And that realization was what had me scared spitless.

I would attend a new school where I didn't know anyone! My best friend, Robin Carter, was spending the year in London. My other best friend—after all, a girl can have more than one best friend—Carrie Giovani was on her way to Rome. Maybe she was already there. I wondered if she was scared. I couldn't imagine Carrie being frightened of anything.

Of course, I hadn't expected to be frightened myself. I tried to draw comfort from the Eiffel Tower—outlined in lights—silhouetted against the night sky. The artist in me appreciated the view. The girl in me longed to see the vast Texas sky, feel the warm Texas breeze against my skin, and pick up the phone to call a friend. But long-distance phone calls were expensive and totally out of the question on a regular basis. Emergency only to friends. Once a week to parents.

I couldn't quite bring myself to classify these jitters as an emergency. Even though I thought I had a good chance of bringing up the foie gras I'd eaten for dinner. The French considered it a real gourmet

2

item. Me, I hadn't been too thrilled when the meal was over to discover I'd wolfed down fatted goose liver.

Absorbing a culture was part of being a Year Abroad student. It required a strong stomach, a stout heart, lots of courage, and a desire for adventure. Robin, Carrie, and I had made a pact to e-mail each other at least once a day in order to keep our morale boosted—and to share these exciting moments.

I glanced around my room. The wallpaper was a mosaic of blues and purples. The host family had to guarantee that a YA student would have her own room. I couldn't believe that this one was so tiny. But that was typical for the French who lived in cities. Small houses or apartments were all this city of over two million people could find room for. Two million people. I could barely comprehend that number. My hometown bragged a population of ten thousand.

This small home had several balconies. Even my room had a balcony. I imagined a romantic French guy climbing the tree outside my room, clambering over the railing of the balcony, and reciting poetry.

Okay, so I was getting a little carried away, but it was hard not to. My bedroom had a canopied bed— so romantic! Even the poster of the Backstreet Boys on the wall sent my romantic yearnings into overdrive. I had a small desk where I'd already set up my laptop computer so I could easily e-mail my friends.

My very own room. Back home in Mustang, Texas, I had to share a room with my younger sister. That hadn't always been the case. Before my parents got divorced, I had my own room, but everything changed with the divorce. My parents had to sell our family home in order to buy two houses—one small one for my mom, my sister, and me and one even smaller for my dad. I resented the divorce sometimes, felt like my parents should have tried harder to keep us together as a family. I thought of all the things we'd have if they'd pooled their money instead of having to purchase two of everything: house, furniture, appliances.

Their divorce had also added to the stress of my getting into the YA program. I'd ask Mom for permission to apply to the program, and she'd tell me to discuss it with my father. Before the divorce, she always called him "your dad." After the divorce, he became "your father." So unfriendly sounding.

When I'd ask my dad about being in the YA program, he'd tell me to talk to my mother. Same thing. Before the divorce, he called her "your mom." Then she became "your mother."

They weren't outwardly mean to each other, and I wasn't irreversibly scarred by the divorce or anything, but those small things told me they weren't in love anymore. And that sorta hurt sometimes.

I was a big believer in love. My first foray into the experience had been with Todd Haskell, and it had been a disaster. I think I wanted to be in love so badly

4

that I convinced myself he was the one, and he turned out to be such a jerk. The final straw had been dumped in my lap the day after Valentine's Day, when he brought me a red-heart-shaped box of chocolates. I'm a sucker for chocolate, especially when it comes in a heart-shaped box with a plastic rose glued on top. But knowing that he'd waited until the day *after* Valentine's Day so he could get it half price made me feel . . . well, unloved. I figured if you really cared about someone, you didn't skimp on the things that counted—like making her feel special.

But Todd was out of my life now, and Paris was in, and with this city came the opportunity to meet, date, and fall in love with a romantic guy. I knew our time together would come to an end when I had to return home after I completed my year abroad.

But until that final moment came, I would know what it was to be loved and romanced. To have someone who was willing to pay full price for my chocolate. I could hardly wait to meet Mr. Romantic.

But before I met the perfect guy, I had to get down to the tedious task of unpacking my clothes.

A knock sounded, and I was grateful for the reprieve. I hurried across the room and opened the door. My host sister, Renée Trouvel, stood in the hallway.

"How's it going?" she asked with a wonderful French accent.

"Très bien," I responded. Very well. I hadn't taken two years of French at Mustang High for nothing.

Renée laughed. She had long, black hair and

dancing blue eyes. "You can practice your French on me, and I'll practice my English on you."

I sagged and smiled wearily. "I'm really too tired to concentrate on French tonight. I wish I'd had a few days to adjust before school started." But a few more days might have just made me more nervous. Besides, I'd enjoyed the layover in London. Carrie, Robin, her host brother, Kit, and I had gone to the Tower of London. And Robin had really needed the support of friends when she realized that Kit was a guy and not a girl. I was still a little worried about her. She had this crazy notion that she wanted to turn into Princess Di while she was in London—instead of just being her wonderful self.

"I haven't even started to unpack," I explained to Renée. "I was too busy admiring the spectacular view through my window."

"Do you not have a view like this from your bedroom at home?" she asked in halting English.

"Are you kidding?" I asked. "Trees, sky, and street-lights—that's about all I can see from my window."

"I thought you would see cactus and horses," she murmured, stepping farther into the room. "You know . . . cowboys."

I smiled warmly. "No cactus where I live. We do have a ranch or two outside of town, but it's probably nothing like you're imagining."

"I must go there someday," she said wistfully.

"Sure. When you visit, you can stay with me," I offered.

I walked to the bed and opened my suitcase. Renée squealed and pulled out one of my denim vests. It had ropes embroidered along the front.

"How cute!" she exclaimed. "A cowboy would wear this."

"I have a lot of western-looking clothes," I told her. "You can wear that one."

Her blue eyes grew really large. "Really?" She hugged the denim to her chest. "*Merci!* But I have nothing to let you wear."

I raised my brows. "Not true. I've been drooling over that miniskirt since I met you at the airport."

"This old thing?" she asked.

This old thing was a deep emerald green skirt that stopped at midthigh. Very chic. I had a lime green sweater that would be perfect with it. Back in Mustang, I'd be wearing shorts to class, but here the weather was already cooler than I was used to.

"Could you teach me how to tie that scarf around my neck?" I inquired. I had been admiring that fashion statement as well.

Renée touched the silk at her throat as if incredibly surprised. I worked part-time in a clothing store, and I figured I should really know how to add the little touches to items of clothing that made them seem so unique, but I'd never quite mastered it. Whenever I tied something, the bow or the knot always looked askew.

"*Oui.* I can teach you," she assured me, her eyes alight. She quickly untied the scarf and slid it from

7

around her neck. "Come to the mirror."

I hurried to the dresser and stood before the mirror, which only showed me from the waist up. I could get to my unpacking later. Renée and I were almost the same height and build. She slipped the scarf around my neck, tied it with a tiny knot, and stepped back. *"Bon."*

Oh, it was *très bon*. With the knot on the side of my throat and the ends flowing over my shoulder, I looked sophisticated. "This is wonderful! Do it more slowly so I can watch."

Laughing, she untied the scarf and started over. She tugged on one end of the scarf. "This end goes on bottom, this end on top. The one on top goes over the one on bottom. Otherwise they both stick up like a bad-hair day."

I giggled. I'd been so afraid that I wouldn't have anything in common with my host sister, and here we were, discussing fashion accessories. She taught me several different ways to arrange the scarf. It was so exciting. Sometimes I even looked like a model. A short model, to be sure, but still a model.

"This will help me so much," I murmured, studying my stylish reflection in the mirror.

Renée wrinkled her brow. "Help you what?"

I hadn't planned to bare my soul so soon, but I felt incredibly comfortable around Renée. I spun around and met her gaze. "If I tell you, you have to promise not to laugh."

She pressed her palm over her heart. "I promise."

8

I took a deep breath and blurted out, "I want to fall in love while I'm in Paris."

"Fall in love?" she repeated.

I nodded quickly. "A year of romance like I'd never get in little Mustang, Texas. I want a guy who doesn't mumble one-word sentences like 'yep' and 'nope.' A guy who doesn't think that 'roses are red, violets are blue' is a romantic poem."

Her mouth fell open. "Are American guys like that?"

I dropped onto the edge of the bed and nodded balefully. "They are in Mustang."

"They know nothing of romance?" she asked, clearly unable to believe it. Her reaction reinforced what I'd already thought—Paris guys knew how to love right.

"They know absolutely nothing," I assured her. "It was a romantic date if my former boyfriend, Todd the Jerk Haskell, belched only three times during the meal."

Laughing, she fell across the bed and raised up an elbow. "I cannot believe this."

"Believe it," I retorted. "This year I want to experience what I will never find in Mustang. Someone who can whisper romantic French phrases into my ear. Someone who knows the art of romance."

I knew that dating a Paris guy would mean heartbreak at the end of the year when we had to say good-bye, but for this one year I would be romanced and cherished just as I had always dreamed.

9

Two

Dana

I STOOD IN front of the mirror the next morning, barely able to believe my eyes. My clothes were still packed, but I'd managed to find my lime green sweater. I was wearing Renée's emerald green skirt and my silver belt that I usually wore with denim, but somehow it looked right with this outfit. And the scarf was tied daintily around my neck. Renée had loaned me a hunter green felt beret. It sat jauntily on top of my red hair.

I'd applied my makeup to perfection so it hid the freckles that dotted the bridge of my nose and the rounded curves of my cheeks. My outfit of varying green shades highlighted the green hue of my eyes. I knew that I was going to turn heads today. By the end of the week Mr. Romance would be walking up to me and whispering those romantic French phrases in my ear.

A knock on the door broke into my fantasy. Renée peered into the room. "We need to eat breakfast and head to school."

I turned around slowly. "What do you think?"

"You look terrific," she assured me.

"I'm as nervous as a dog dreamin' of catchin' a rabbit," I confessed.

She laughed. "You Americans have the funniest sayings."

I smiled. "That's probably more Texan than American," I admitted.

"Even so, you don't look nervous," she told me.

I grabbed my backpack and followed her into the hallway. "I'm only going to be here a year, so it's important that I impress some guy right away," I explained.

"Love takes time," she muttered.

"I don't have time," I emphasized as we went down the stairs. Besides, I wasn't looking for an until-death-do-us-part kind of love. I only wanted romance.

"Bonjour!" Madame Trouvel said when we walked into the small kitchen. It looked much like our kitchen in Mustang. Tile-covered counters, cupboards, an island that resembled a butcher's block in the middle. *"Comment allez-vous,* Dana?"

How are you? *"Très bien,"* I assured my host mother.

"Wonderful! Sit down and eat," she ordered.

Monsieur Trouvel and Renée's sister, Geneviève, joined us. Geneviève was two years younger than Renée, and in a way she reminded me of my sister,

11

Marci. I hadn't expected to miss Marci. We fought more often than we agreed, but I guess that's what sisters are for.

I brought a blue bowl-shaped cup to my mouth and sipped café au lait. Basically it's coffee with a generous amount of milk. It warmed me, chasing away the chill of dread that was trying to creep over me. I dug into my food. If I concentrated on the moment and didn't think about the future, I thought I might make it to school without throwing up.

"Are you ready for your first day at Renée's school?" Monsieur Trouvel prodded.

So much for concentrating on the moment. My stomach knotted up at the reminder, and I knew I was finished with breakfast. I smiled kindly at Renée's father. He had dark hair like Renée and the same deep blue eyes. I hadn't expected it to be so hard to sit at a table with a complete family. "As ready as I'll ever be."

With apprehension mounting, I walked through the halls of the lycée—the French equivalent of Mustang High with a little twist. Only the top students attended. They were preparing to take the baccalaureate exams that would determine whether or not they could go to the university.

On my way to my first class I realized that I really wasn't ready for my first day at a Paris school. It was more than nerves and jitters. It was a complete lack of knowledge. I felt like I'd been dropped off on an alien planet and told, "Good luck!" just before the spaceship abandoned me.

Renée had taken me to the main office to get my schedule, my locker number, and a map of the school, showing where different classes were. Unfortunately, all the directions were written in French.

Yeah, sure, I'd had two years of French, and if someone spoke really slowly and had a slight Texas drawl, I could usually figure out what he or she was saying, but the people here didn't talk slowly, and they definitely didn't have a Texas drawl.

I don't know why I'd expected people to talk in English with a French accent. I couldn't figure out why I hadn't realized that they actually *spoke* French in France!

I guess that was the reason French guys could spout romantic French words. They talked French all the time!

I was beginning to wish I had studied more diligently in my French class back home instead of always doodling. But my hands had a life of their own, always drawing, always sketching. It was a given that if I had pencil and paper, I was going to draw something.

As I headed toward class—sculpting—I was a bit disconcerted to notice that people were paired up or grouped like friends. Renée had been wonderful showing me around, but she'd had to skedaddle to get to her math class, and it was obvious that they

13

had cliques here—just like at home—and right now I didn't belong.

But I planned to belong and the sooner, the better. I could see guys checking me out, and I was definitely giving them a once-over.

I had developed a point system based on looks, attitude, cool clothes, smile, and a whole host of other attributes. Right now I was just making mental tallies because I didn't want to be obvious by pulling out my little notepad and taking copious notes.

With mounting anticipation, I spotted the doorway that led into my first class. This was it. The moment I had anticipated for months. I could hardly wait to sit beside the cutest French guy in the class, introduce myself in my practiced French phrases, and begin my journey toward romance.

Taking a deep breath, I stepped into the room and staggered to a stop.

No way! my mind screamed. *No way!* I was hallucinating. Having a flashback. Experiencing déjà vu. Or maybe my mind simply refused to accept that I was actually in Paris. It thought I was still in Mustang, Texas!

That was the only logical explanation. I blinked several times, but the tabloid remained unchanged. Horrifying. Excruciatingly painful, even. The last thing in the world that I wanted.

Blinking wasn't working to erase the image before me. Closing my eyes, I gave my head a quick shake. I thought of an Etch A Sketch. I just wanted to obliterate the image, wipe it from existence.

When I opened my eyes, to my profound disappointment, nothing had changed.

The room had tables, two chairs to a table. Only one chair was vacant. I couldn't believe this! One chair. The chair I would have to sit in.

One solitary chair—right beside a guy with brown hair. A guy I recognized! A guy from my high school back home.

What in the world was Alex Turner Johnson doing here?

Three

Dana

"TRYING TO CATCH flies?" Alex asked.

I snapped my mouth shut. To my absolute mortification I realized that I'd been staring at him, and he'd been rude enough not only to notice but to comment on it. So typically Mustang, Texas.

Because I had no choice, I walked toward him as if I was going to my execution. I absolutely did not want to sit by someone who spoke with a Texas accent. I dropped into the chair beside him. "What are you doing here?" I demanded.

He shrugged. "Waiting for the nude models to arrive."

I was afraid that the hinges on my jaws were going to lock up because of the way my mouth kept dropping open. I knew my eyes very nearly popped out of my head. *Nude models?*

16

I had expected school in Paris to be different from school in Mustang. Paris was renowned for its artwork. Much of that work involved people in what my grandmother referred to as their birthday suits, but I hadn't expected to jump into a project this intense on the first day. I felt heat suffuse my face, and I had to know. "Male or female?"

"Both," he replied in a way that made me think he was on the verge of yawning.

I couldn't believe how calmly Alex had responded. As if the most scandalous event in our young lives wasn't about to occur. I'd seen guys on the beach in skimpy swimsuits that didn't leave a lot to the imagination, but to see in the flesh what I hadn't even dared to dream about—and to see it for the first time in front of a whole class . . . with people I didn't know sitting around me. . . . No, wait, it was worse than that. I was sitting by someone who did know me, and for some reason that had my face burning even hotter. We'd both be sitting here side by side, gazing at . . .

Alex averted his face and pressed a fist to his mouth. His shoulders were jerking like a spastic chicken as he tried to contain his laughter. I narrowed my eyes, the anger roiling through me. "You're lying!" I accused.

He choked back his laughter.

"You believed me. You are so gullible," he chortled.

With my fist I pounded his shoulder, surprised

17

that it didn't have any give to it. The guy didn't play football on the Mustang High football team, so I'd expected him to be flab without an ounce of brawn.

"You creep," I retorted. His joking around was so typical of the immature guys in Mustang. Thank goodness I was going to be spared their presence in abundance this year. If only I'd had the good fortune to be spared his at this moment. "How did someone as immature as you get accepted into the YA program anyway?"

He stopped laughing and poked his finger into the mound of clay that sat on the table in front of him. "My parents pulled a few strings."

"I didn't even know you'd applied for the program," I murmured. I certainly didn't remember seeing him at any of the information meetings that had been held before and after the selections were made.

"It was a last-minute thing." He broke off a piece of clay and began to roll it between his fingers. He had really long fingers, and his nails were evenly clipped, not chipped or broken. I'd learned early on not to wear anything with threads that might get caught and snagged by one of Todd the Jerk Haskell's hangnails. His idea of a manicure had been to pull out his trusty pocketknife.

"You weren't on our flight—"

"Like I said, it was last minute," he interrupted, obviously annoyed. "That particular flight was already booked solid, so I had to take another one."

"Excuse me for pretending to care," I shot back.

He glanced at his watch and heaved a sigh. "This class is going to be over before it even gets started."

As if that was his cue, the teacher strolled into the room. His graying hair was pulled back into a ponytail that curled at his waist. Definitely not the style the male teachers at Mustang High wore.

And then my worst nightmare began. He began to speak—in French. Rapidly.

"Je ne comprends pas," I murmured. I don't understand. Panic seized me. I considered raising my hand and repeating myself, asking for a bit of leniency here, wanting him to issue his orders a little more slowly.

But as I glanced hastily around the room, it became obvious that I was the only one with a problem. Students were starting to work their fingers into the clay. I decided to take my cue from them. The clay had a really smooth texture. It was almost a sensual experience to knead the clay with my palms.

I darted a quick glance at Alex. He not only had long fingers, but he had large hands. They practically swallowed the clay as he shaped and molded it. His face was set in absolute concentration. It almost looked like he was trying to breathe life into the blob in front of him.

I imagined those hands caressing my cheek, massaging my neck and shoulders—whoa!

Where did that thought come from?

The last thing I wanted was for someone from

Mustang, Texas, to fulfill my fantasies for a romantic year in Paris. And I absolutely did not want Alex running his hands amok over my back.

No. I wanted someone else. A French guy.

As discreetly as I could because I didn't want Alex to know what I was up to, I studied the guys in the class.

Blonds, brunets, even a redhead. They all looked pretty serious about their project. That got them an extra point. Since art was my life, I wanted a guy who could relate, someone I could talk to about artistic endeavors.

There were a couple of really hot guys. I gave a total of twelve points for looks, and both of those guys got full credit. They were much cuter than dull Alex from Mustang. With his hair the color of mud and his soulful, brown eyes.

Tomorrow I would definitely have to get to class early so I could have the opportunity to sit by a Frenchie. This class had promise, lots of promise.

And none of those promises involved Alex Turner Johnson.

Four

Alex

DANA MADISON HAD the most delicate, elegant hands I'd ever seen. Just like a girl, she prodded the clay like she thought it would bite. Me, I was enjoying the texture of the clay and grateful for the opportunity to pound my fists into something, to squeeze and tear apart a blob. That gray goo represented my life. My life had no shape, no texture, no color.

I didn't usually have such a dreary outlook. As a matter of fact, until six weeks ago, when my parents announced that they'd enrolled me in the Year Abroad program, I'd say for the most part, I was a pretty happy guy. I'd dated a little, had good grades, and had plans for college that included a career path that would lead me straight into animated movies, working for Pixar.

Then my parents had dropped the bomb. They were getting a divorce and thought it would go easier on me if I wasn't at home while they "went through it." As if my being thousands of miles away would spare me the pain of our family falling apart.

I slammed my fist into the clay, and the table wobbled. Dana screeched and jerked back in her chair, her eyes wide.

"Gently, Monsieur Turner," the teacher scolded. I felt my entire face burn with embarrassment. "I realize that Americans are crude, but in my class you must pretend you are French."

Great, I thought. *A bigot.* I had discovered that Americans weren't real popular in Paris.

"What's wrong?" Dana whispered. "And why does he call you Monsieur *Turner* instead of Monsieur Johnson?"

I shoved the clay aside. "I'm going by my middle name while I'm here—three names is a lot in a foreign country." I didn't have to get into the whole divorce thing and how upset I was about it. "What's wrong is that this is a stupid class and a total waste of my time." I grabbed my backpack and stormed into the hallway. I turned the corner and pressed my back against the brick wall. I plowed my fingers through my hair. *That was real smart, Turner. I think your grades here transfer back home. You gotta make the best of this, dude, no matter how much you dislike being here.*

And making the best of it, in my opinion, meant getting heavily involved with a French babe.

22

Physical only. No emotion. No bonding. No declarations of love.

I stood in the hallway for a long time, trying to gain control over my anger and frustration. This year had barely begun, and already I hated it to the max.

The bell finally rang, and I began wandering the hall, heading for my next class. Oils. Nothing to punch, plenty to smear. For some reason, I thought of the finger painting I did as a kid. A mess of colors that made no sense, that represented nothing. Just like my life.

I shook my head to clear it as I walked into the class and took my place behind an easel. I didn't want to think about my life, or my parents' lives, or my older brother, Peter's, life. Peter was no longer living at home. He'd started going to the University of Texas last year. But my parents couldn't wait until I started college. Oh no. *Let's send Alex off to Paris so we can go ahead and get a divorce. So what if this decision ruins his last two years of high school?* My own personal way of acting out was to drop the Johnson, at least while I was in France. Three names *was* a lot to say to people who didn't speak your language. My parents didn't know—and they wouldn't have to know.

While I'd been brooding, the class had filled up quickly. And who should stroll in just as the bell rang?

Dana Madison. I couldn't believe it. Of all the schools in all of Paris, how in the world did she end up enrolled in mine? And worse than that, how had she managed to get herself into two of my classes?

Her presence here was a nightmare. I did not need—nor did I want—someone from my high school back home dogging my steps. And as fate would have it, she was late again and the only easel left was the one beside me. I'd hoped it would go to one of the French girls, but my thunderous scowl had probably chased them all away. I was going to have to watch that expression.

"Can't you get anywhere on time?" I chided as she came to sit on the stool beside mine.

"I'm having a hard time figuring out the French," she admitted, setting her backpack on the floor.

"Well, duh! This is France. What did you expect?" I retorted.

"Give me a break, will you? I don't want to sit beside you any more than you want to sit beside me," she snapped.

Ouch! That hurt. Normally it wouldn't have. Normally it would have washed right over me like the proverbial water off a duck's back. But nothing in my life had been normal since my parents' earth-shattering announcement.

I knew Dana didn't mean to reject my presence, to reject me—I didn't even know why I cared. Yes, I did. I just didn't want to think about it.

No matter how many times my parents told me that their divorce wasn't my fault, I couldn't help but think that it was. I needed a major distraction. I needed to get involved with a French babe, someone I couldn't understand, someone I wouldn't grow to love. A flash of passion, hot kisses; that's all I wanted. Nothing permanent. Just someone I could lose myself with so I could forget my parents' divorce. A French girl would be perfect for that ploy.

Sure, she'd be temporary, just for a year, but that was fine with me because the one thing I'd learned lately was that love didn't last.

The teacher, Mademoiselle Etiènne, was sweeping her paintbrush across the canvas, demonstrating the mastery of stroke. Her back was to the class, which I found incredibly convenient.

I allowed my gaze to wander around the room, weighing the merits of the female students. Eventually my gaze completed its circle and fell on Dana.

Shafts of sunlight streaked through the windows to highlight her red hair. Her hair was a shade that I couldn't describe, had never before envisioned. Did I even have that color available in my palette?

And her green eyes—like green in the spring. The gentle buds of a new leaf reaching for the sun.

She was so absorbed in what the teacher was saying, so totally captivated. And captivating.

She shifted her gaze to me. I jerked my attention to the teacher. The last thing I was interested in was having a relationship with someone from back home.

I headed for a nearby café as soon as I gathered my books from my locker after the four-thirty bell rang—signaling the end of the day. Apparently everyone else had the same plan. The line of patrons waiting to be served was half a block long. People were crammed inside the shop, and all the outside tables—with their bright red-and-yellow umbrellas open to shield the patrons from the sun—were full.

My stomach growled, and I patted it. "Sorry, old buddy," I mumbled. I was famished and figured I'd faint from hunger before I ever got a table. I'd have to seek out other means to tame this rabid starving beast.

Just as I turned to go, I saw a familiar face. Dana! Sitting alone at a table beneath an umbrella. Relief swept through me. My stomach was going to be saved from a fate worse than death after all.

I wended my way through the crowd and wove among the tables until I reached Dana. I dropped into the empty chair across from her.

"You finally got someplace early," I said as I snatched the menu from her fingers.

"You can't sit there!" she shrieked.

"Why not? I'm starving, and it's empty," I pointed out, my mouth already watering as I considered the options on the menu.

"I'm saving it for someone," she responded.

I scoffed. "Yeah, right." After only one day in school, who could she possibly know?

Leaning forward, she grabbed the menu from my fingers. "I'm meeting Renée," she insisted.

Renée? In France, Renée was a guy's name, wasn't it?

So what if it was? What did I care if she was

already dating? But oddly, it bugged me.

"Is this guy in one of your classes?" I asked, trying to sound uninterested, wondering why I had to try when I *was* totally uninterested.

Something that reminded me of the cunning look of a fox filled her eyes.

She tossed her head, the kind of move that a girl with long hair would make. I wondered briefly if she'd forgotten that her hair was short.

"No, I met Renée shortly after my flight touched down. We had an instant rapport. As a matter of fact, we were together last night until after midnight."

I really didn't want to hear about her date with some Frenchie. I figured I should probably move to a table with a Parisian girl, where I wouldn't have to worry about conversation. I glanced around. The place was packed like a can of sardines. It was either this table or the line.

I leaned forward and held out a hand imploringly. "Look, Dana, I'm starving. I missed lunch."

She quirked a delicate brow.

I grimaced. "All right. I'm having a hard time reading the French too. I couldn't find the cafeteria."

A bubble of laughter erupted from her throat. For some reason, it made me want to laugh, and I hadn't felt like laughing in over six weeks.

"Come on—just let me place an order," I pleaded, clasping my hands and shaking them in front of her. "I'll wolf it down and be out of here before this René guy ever shows up. Have pity. I'm a stranger in a strange land."

She laughed harder. She had a really pretty laugh. Light and airy. It kept washing over me in waves.

"Please," I begged. "Please." I began to gasp and rasp like a man crawling across the desert. "I'm starving. Food. I need food. *Le menu, s'il te plaît.*"

She thrust the menu at me. "You're pathetic. People are staring."

"*Merci,* mademoiselle." Triumphant, I leaned back and studied the menu. When the waitress came over, I ordered a couple of sandwiches. I wasn't certain what was in them and didn't want to drag out my English-French dictionary in front of Dana. I knew the bread was a croissant. I just hoped whatever fixings came in the middle weren't going to make me regret trying to act like I wasn't an ignorant tourist.

I watched Dana sip something that looked like lemonade but probably wasn't. I didn't remember her being so cute back in Mustang. I cleared my throat. "So how does Todd feel about you being all the way over here?"

Her green eyes popped open wide. "Why would I care?"

I felt the heat rush to my face. "I thought the two of you were an item."

"A discarded item," she responded.

"Hey, I'm sorry."

She held up a hand. "Don't be. When you start

28

at the bottom of the food chain, the only place to go is up."

I fought back a smile. I never had been able to figure out what she saw in the guy anyway. I mean, he wasn't an absolute loser, but the guy seemed more obsessed with riding bulls than dating. He was severely bowlegged.

"I didn't know you had an interest in art," I remarked. She'd been in my sketching class as well that afternoon. That gave us three classes together. Fortunately in the sketching class, though, someone had taken the chair beside me before Dana arrived, so I was spared her nearness as Madame Trudi explained the process of sketching and gave us our first assignment.

"I always took art as my elective at Mustang High." She furrowed her brow. "I don't remember having you in any art classes."

"Are you kidding?" I inquired. "And have the guys think I was a pansy?" I leaned forward conspiratorially. "So let's just keep my little foray into the art world between us when we get back home, okay?"

"No one would think you were a pansy," she insisted.

"Yeah, right. Most of the guys at Mustang think a smiley face is a work of art."

She giggled. Man, I liked that sound.

"That is so true," she responded.

"I mean, the guys are either into football or riding bulls, and the really macho guys do both," I explained.

29

"I can't see you on a bull," she commented. "But I could see you on the football team."

I sighed heavily. "My mom had a friend who played college football. He got tackled, snapped his neck, and was paralyzed. My mom forbid me or my brother to play football."

Dana furrowed her brow. "Her friend's accident must have been hard for your mom. I can certainly understand where she's coming from. Still, there's basketball, baseball, and track."

I shook my head. "No time for school sports."

"You make time for what's important," she pointed out.

"Exactly." I leaned back as the waitress set my sandwiches in front of me. "And school sports are not important to me."

Gingerly I lifted the top of one sandwich and peered at its insides.

"Don't know what you ordered, do you?" she teased.

"Yeah, I know what I ordered. Croissant sandwiches. I just don't know what's between the layers of bread," I confessed.

She laughed again, that remarkable laugh.

I bit into the sandwich, grateful to discover it was turkey.

"Uh, listen," she began hesitantly.

I finished chewing and swallowed. She looked really uncomfortable, and for one horrifying moment I was afraid that she knew about my parents' divorce. I'd been too ashamed to tell anyone, but in a small town like Mustang, gossip can spread like a brushfire.

With the tip of her elegant finger, she wiped the dew off her glass. "We had to put our clay projects on a table at the back of the room. I put yours away. It'll be easy for you to find tomorrow. It's the one that's not even beginning to look like anything yet."

Guilt pricked my conscience. "Ah, man, thanks. I really appreciate you doing that for me. I'm sorry I went postal—"

She held up a hand. "I understand completely."

Huh? How could she? Unless she knows about the divorce.

"I didn't expect it to be so hard to adjust to a new school, a new city, and a new family either," she added.

"Yeah." *A new family,* I thought. Once I adjusted here, I'd have to adjust back home. "I think all the classes are pretty good," I added, wanting to shift the subject away from my adjustments. I didn't know if I ever would adjust to my life A.D. After Divorce.

"I was surprised that we already have an assignment in sketching class," she admitted. "What are you going to sketch?"

"The Eiffel Tower," I said without hesitation.

She rolled her eyes. "That is so expected. So boring."

Before I had a chance to tell her my complete plans for the sketch, a girl with long, black hair and blue eyes dragged over a chair from another table and joined us.

31

"Hi, Renée," Dana said. "Meet Alex Turner from Mustang High."

Renée was a girl? I'd been deceived. Dana had knowingly let me believe Renée was a guy.

Dana looked incredibly cute with her smug expression. I had a feeling she was paying me back for my nude-model prank in our first class. She'd been cute then too and so obviously horrified at the thought of looking at a nude model.

I'd felt almost guilty about teasing her.

I could tell now that she had enjoyed my initial baffled expression, enjoyed more the fact that I realized I'd been had.

She'd tilted up her nose, and her eyes were challenging me to admit I'd fallen for her ploy, hook, line, and sinker.

I hadn't known Dana well back in Mustang, and now I was wondering why I'd paid so little attention to her there. She was intriguing.

Whoa! I didn't want to travel that route.

My goal this year was a French babe. Not some girl from Mustang High.

Five

Dana

IABSOLUTELY COULD not believe the way Renée flirted with Alex—like he was something special!

Obviously it was a case of not realizing what you have. Renée was surrounded by romantic French guys all the time, so I figured she found Alex intriguing simply because of the fact that he was so utterly boring.

And a liar! He'd apparently forgotten his promise to wolf down his food and hightail it out of there. I really wanted to talk to Renée about the best place to meet guys. And I absolutely could not do that with Alex in attendance. No way.

I tapped my fingers impatiently on the table, but the guy didn't seem to be taking the hint. Dense. So completely dense.

I couldn't believe that he'd actually made me

laugh with his confession, reluctantly given, that he was having a hard time understanding the French and then the way he'd looked at that sandwich—fear clearly etched in his face.

I hadn't spent much time talking to Alex at Mustang. We'd had a class or two together, and we'd occasionally said hi when we passed in the hallway—if we weren't talking to someone else at the time.

But I really didn't know much about him. And didn't want to.

I certainly didn't want to spend my year abroad getting chummy with Alex Turner Johnson—or just plain Alex Turner as he wanted to be called—when there were romantic French guys to while away the hours with.

"Football games," he murmured, shoving his crumb-filled plate aside and smiling at Renée. "I think I'll miss the Friday night football games the most."

Was he trying to do a number on her, impress her with an athletic ability he didn't possess? "You don't play football," I pointed out.

He jerked his gaze to me. "I watch the games."

Oh, right. Why had I been so quick to jump on his case? Because he was interfering with my goal. Still, I couldn't stop myself from commenting, "I already miss the football games."

Alex looked at Renée, his eyes sparkling with excitement. "There's nothing like a game on a cold night."

"With a blanket draped around you and your best friends, all of you snuggling close," I added, thinking of all the Friday nights I had sat huddled between Carrie and Robin. We'd yelled at the top of our lungs until we were hoarse while the Mustang High Mustangs had made us proud. We'd drunk hot chocolate from a thermos.

"Remember last year's homecoming game?" Alex asked.

My heart actually began to pound, and I could hear the crowds. "Who could forget that?" I enthused. I touched Renée's hand. "The score was twelve to fourteen with forty-eight seconds left in the game. We were behind."

"And the opposing team had the ball," Alex said excitedly.

I couldn't believe how cute Alex was when he was talking about something he enjoyed. Something I enjoyed as well.

"And they fumbled!" I cried, trying to distract myself from the glow in his eyes.

"Jackson Lamont ran the ball down," Alex explained.

We both threw our arms in the air and yelled, "Touchdown!"

Heat suffused my face. Alex turned red and averted his gaze. People were staring at us. Renée was laughing.

"I can see why you miss it," she said.

"Uh, yeah . . . w-well," Alex stammered, reaching down and grabbing his backpack. "I gotta go. Thanks for letting me share your table."

He beat a hasty retreat, and was I ever glad. I was certain it was just shared memories that were causing this warm flood of feelings I had toward him. I couldn't like him—well, I could like him—but not in *that* way. Not like the image that suddenly hit me.

Alex Turner and I sitting on a cold metal bench wrapped in a blanket, snuggling close, at a football game!

The Musée du Louvre.

I was thrilled when Renée suggested that we visit the museum. I figured guys interested in art would frequent the place. Cute French guys. It was the perfect place to guy watch.

I was grateful that Renée had made the suggestion after Alex left the café. I was beginning to despair, afraid the guy would never finish eating. Three classes with Alex were enough—a meal with him almost too much.

Sure, I had enjoyed talking about home, but I didn't plan to spend the most monumental year of my life hanging out with someone from Mustang. I'd done that for sixteen years. Enough, already. Now I needed a break. And more, I needed a romantic Paris guy.

And where better to look than an art museum?

One of the most romantic things about Paris in my opinion was the abundance of gardens. They were beautiful and everywhere. Le Jardin des Tuileries surrounds the Louvre. French landscaping is an art form, and I realized these magnificent gardens were no exception as we walked through them on our way to the Louvre.

The museum itself was fascinating beyond my wildest dreams. It dated back to medieval times, and French kings had constantly renovated it and built onto it until it was huge: a myriad of buildings, 140 exhibition rooms, and eight miles of galleries.

As we wandered from room to room, I felt like I was in heaven—artist heaven. The art collection was incredible, the most important in the world. I found myself staring at original masterpieces like Leonardo da Vinci's *Mona Lisa* and forgetting my mission: to scout out the guys.

I imagined strolling through the Louvre with a guy who could actually appreciate all this. Todd's idea of artwork was stick figures.

Renée and I were engrossed in a sculpture titled *The Dying Slave*. A work by Michelangelo.

"I wouldn't mind meeting the guy who posed for this," I whispered to Renée.

"I think he is long dead," Renée whispered back.

"I'll settle for one of his descendants," I told her.

She smiled. "You think he would be romantic?"

"Well, let's see." I reached into my backpack and pulled out my notebook. "I have a ranking system. Zero is absolute loser in that area. Three is the best. So what should we give this guy for hair?"

She laughed lightly. "Since he seems to have plenty, I guess a three."

"I agree. Eyes, I'll have to give him a two because I don't know what color they are." The marble statue was all white. "I think blue is the most romantic."

"Eye color is romantic?" she asked, clearly amused.

"Sure. For physique, this guy definitely gets a three. Then I have personality broken down. Humor?" I allowed my gaze to wander over the statue.

"Well," Renée murmured. "He's not smiling."

What in the world would a dying slave have to smile about? Still, I thought he appeared stoic. "Okay. I'll give him a one. Intelligence?"

"Hard to say."

"Romantic?"

"Very!" we both said at the same time, and giggled. All in all, I knew I wouldn't be dating the statue. But this little exercise was demonstrating that using my point system wasn't going to be the perfect solution. A lot of things you didn't discover until it was too late—just as I had with Todd.

"Come on," I urged. "Let's find some real guys to evaluate."

We began walking toward the next room.

"I'm not sure love should be based on points," Renée explained.

"That's because you live in a world of romantic guys," I declared as we neared the doorway. "I only have this year to enjoy romance, so I have to find the best-possible guy. The one who can fulfill all my fantasies."

Out of the corner of my eye I saw a really cute guy. Tall. Blond. I made notations in my notebook, thinking he might be worth introducing myself to. I glanced back over my shoulder at him. Definitely hot.

Wham!

Someone rammed into me—or I rammed into him. My notebook and pencil went flying out of my hands, landing on the floor with a thud and a ping. Strong hands wrapped around my arms and steadied me. I jerked back my head.

To my horror, I was staring at Alex Turner.

"You okay?" he asked.

"Why don't you watch where you're going?" I snapped, even though I was the one who hadn't been watching.

"Sorry. I'm having a hard time dragging my gaze from the statues." He bent down and picked up my notebook and pencil. He furrowed his brow. "Why are you working a math problem when you're surrounded by all this exquisite artwork?"

I snatched my notebook from his fingers. "It's none of your business." His brow creased more deeply, and I didn't want him figuring out what my *math problem* really was. I decided to change the subject quickly. "Are you here to get ideas for your art project—something other than the predictable Eiffel Tower?"

"No, I'm definitely doing the tower," he insisted.

This guy was incredibly unimaginative. "That is so boring!"

"It's a Paris landmark."

"Exactly," I pointed out. "Don't you think it's been done a thousand times?"

"Not the way I'm going to do it," he insisted.

"What? Are you going to try and imitate Picasso?" I chided.

"No, it'll be an original Turner, which means it'll have a unique perspective."

"Oh yeah, right," I scoffed.

"Why don't you come with me tomorrow after school to the place where I plan to sketch the tower?" he challenged, a formidable glint in his eyes.

I love challenges, and for some reason, I really wanted to prove to this guy that he was as uninspiring as our hometown. I gave him a cocky smile. "Okay."

"Great," he replied, although he didn't sound like he really thought it was great. He was probably already having second thoughts because he realized how mundane his sketch would be—and I'd witness that revelation.

"I'll catch up with you tomorrow," he said just before he turned on his heel and walked away.

With a sinking feeling in the pit of my stomach, it hit me exactly what I'd agreed to do.

My first date in Paris was with an American, a boring American from Mustang!

Six

Dana

I TOSSED THE clothes from my suitcase into the dresser drawers. If I didn't keep my hands busy, I would pull out my hair. I couldn't believe that I'd actually agreed to go somewhere with Alex Turner.

What had I been thinking? Obviously I hadn't been thinking.

He was so smug about his desire to draw the Eiffel Tower. I guess I wanted to be present when he realized that I was right and he was so totally wrong.

That was a lousy reason. Why did I care what he drew? I didn't. I didn't care anything about him. I wasn't interested in him. If he flew home tomorrow, my life would be complete.

I slammed a drawer shut just as someone knocked on my door. Renée walked in and plopped onto my bed. "So tell me everything about Alex," she demanded.

I zipped up my suitcase and moved it to the floor so I could sit on the edge of the mattress. "What do you care? You have a boyfriend."

"Jean-Claude is wonderful, *oui*, but I am fascinated by this Alex," she commented. "He is the first American guy I have ever talked to."

My eyes almost popped out of my head. "Fascinated? He is so uninteresting."

She shrugged and flipped her long, black hair over her shoulder. "I thought he was cute. What scores would you give him with your rating system?"

"All zeros." But even as I spoke, I knew I was lying.

"Come on. Let's see how he rates," she prodded.

"It doesn't matter how he rates," I pointed out. "He isn't French."

"Afraid you'll discover he has a good score?" she challenged.

Sneering—half jokingly—I reached for my notepad and pencil. I stretched out on my stomach. Renée rolled over so our shoulders touched. For a brief moment I thought of Robin and Carrie—and all the times we'd lain on the bed together like this, looking through teen magazines or our high-school yearbooks.

"Eyes?" Renée asked.

"Well, as a rule, I only give a three to blue eyes. . . ." But Alex had eyes the color of melted chocolate, and I

42

was a sucker for chocolate. So I generously gave him a three.

"Smile?" Renée prodded.

"It's imperfect," I stated, my pencil hovering over the paper. His smile was lopsided. The right side always went up higher than the left. It was kind of intriguing, made him look a little shy. I put a three in the smile column.

He had smothered his laughter in class, so I couldn't rate it fairly. Hair. Brown like the mud in a creek back home. Two. I erased the two. He wore it short, and it never looked messed up. Three. I thought of what it would feel like to run my fingers through it. I didn't like how much that thought appealed to me. I erased the three and put back the two.

"What are you doing?" Renée asked.

"Trying to be objective." But the task seemed almost impossible.

I had to give him a one for temper after his angry display in sculpting class that day. A three for manners since he'd included Renée in our conversation and he'd picked up my notebook and pencil when I dropped them. He liked art. Three. Intelligent. Three. It stood to reason that anyone who appreciated art was intelligent. Romantic. A big, fat zero.

I smiled triumphantly. Where it counted the most, he was an absolute loser.

"He'll never do," I commented.

"Are you looking for someone with perfect scores?" Renée asked.

"You bet," I confirmed. "And French."

"Want to double-date?" Renée suddenly asked.

I laughed lightly. "I haven't found Mr. Romantic yet, but when I do—"

"A practice date," she interrupted. "So you can get used to the French dating scene."

"I'm not sure who I'd ask," I confided.

"I could have my boyfriend ask one of his friends to take you out," she offered.

Quickly I sat up. "Do you think he'd do that?"

She grinned. "*Oui.* Jean-Claude is very romantic. He'll find someone good for you."

"This will be great!" I told her. "I really don't want to blow it when I discover the real thing, and Todd wasn't exactly good practice material for how a date should be handled."

As we began discussing possibilities, I turned over my notepad. It bothered me to look at Alex's scores, confused me to even think about him.

The next morning I arrived at sculpting class early. I quickly scouted the room and took a seat beside an absolute dream guy. Blond and blue-eyed, he was the complete opposite of Alex. So his score shot up before I'd even finished assessing him.

He didn't have Alex's broad shoulders or Alex's height, but that was okay. He was French.

He took my hand and kissed my fingers. "*Ma chère,* welcome to Paris."

44

I was melting. How romantic. *"M-Merci,"* I stammered.

Great going, Dana. Impress the guy with your lack of sophistication. There were times when I really resented coming from a small town.

"I'm Dana Madison," I told him.

He smiled, a three-point smile. "We all know who you are. I am Pierre Robards."

I repeated his name. It was fantastic, not dull sounding like Alex.

I glanced over my shoulder, and who should I see but the bane of my existence. Alex Turner was talking with a beautiful French girl, making the girl laugh like a hyena. Good, maybe he'd cancel on this afternoon. I was accustomed to guys bailing at the last minute. Todd had repeatedly done that. If one of the guys called with a better offer than a night out with his girl—like driving trucks through mud—he was there.

I knew instinctively that French guys would be too romantic to cancel a date—for any reason. Although I would be here for only a year, I knew whoever I settled my heart on would follow me back to Texas, would swim the Atlantic and the Gulf of Mexico in order to be with me.

So maybe I had an overactive imagination where love was concerned. I mean, I understood that he wouldn't actually follow me across an ocean. But he would be romantic, and he would give me a year that I could hold close for the rest of my life.

45

"Messieurs! Mesdemoiselles!" The teacher tapped his knuckles on the desk. Then he told us in perfect French that we had to sit in the chair we had sat in yesterday. His seating chart was made.

My stomach dropped to the floor. I wanted to stay where I was. I was on the verge of offering Monsieur Henri an eraser or some Wite-Out when he snapped, *"Vite! Vite!"*

Hurry! Hurry!

I trudged to the table where Alex sat and dropped into the chair beside him.

With a wide grin, he leaned over. He jabbed his thumb over his shoulder. "Pierre over there? Before class, I saw him in the hall with a lip lock on some girl—" He shook his head. "Man, they probably had to bring in the Jaws of Life to separate them so they could get to class."

Disappointment hit me hard. "He has a girlfriend?"

"Either that or they say howdy different over here."

"They do say howdy differently," I shot back, wanting to wipe that smirk off his face. "They say *bonjour*."

I was fuming. Not so much because Pierre had a girlfriend, but because Alex had witnessed my mooning over a guy who was unavailable. I was allowed to make mistakes. I just didn't want Alex Turner to witness them—or more, to comment on them. For all I knew, the girl he'd been talking with might have been lip locked before class as well.

With anger still too close to the surface, I started to mold the clay, working to finish up the project

46

I'd started yesterday—a vase. Unfortunately, it looked more like a lopsided bowl.

"Hey, by the way," Alex whispered conspiratorially.

Startled that he had leaned close enough for me to feel his warm breath skim my neck and to have that same breath send a shiver along my spine, I crumbled one side of my project. Great! Just great. Now I'd have to rebuild. I hadn't planned to have someone from my school back home witness any mistakes I made.

"You're gonna need a bike for our excursion this afternoon," he added.

I glared at him. "Where am I supposed to get a bike?"

"Check with your host sister," he suggested calmly.

"Think you could have told me sooner?" I asked.

"I'm telling you now," he pointed out. "You've got all day to find a bike."

Just like a guy not to realize all that was involved in going out. They never got ready for things. They just went as they were.

Why in the heck couldn't Alex Turner have gone to London like my friend Robin or Rome like my friend Carrie? Why Paris, where he could torment me without even trying?

After school I went straight to my host home. I'd seen Renée at lunch, and she'd told me that I could use her bicycle. How typical of a guy to remember at the last moment that a girl needed to prepare for a date.

47

Whoa! I stopped that thought. This excursion, as Alex called it, was not a date. No way. We were just going to work on our project for sketching class. Hopefully I could find something other than the Eiffel Tower to sketch. I refused to be boring Dana from dull Mustang.

But before I went on the field trip to Ho-hum or wherever Alex planned to go, I needed to get psyched up. And my best friends were the greatest at helping me accomplish that goal.

We'd finally figured out how to get into a private chat room. It was almost like talking on the phone, only our fingers did all the work. I sat at my desk, turned on my computer, logged on to the Internet, and accessed our private room. They were there and waiting.

Dana: *Hey, guys!*
Robin: *Dana! Good to see you! :)*
Carrie: *Dana, how is Paris?*
Dana: *Paris is beautiful. How is Rome?*
Carrie: *Interesting. I'm engaged in a little experiment with a guy named Antonio.*
Robin: *What kind of experiment?*
Carrie: *Teaching him a lesson. Unfortunately, the better I know him, the more I'm regretting this brilliant idea I had. He hates Americans. And he doesn't know I'm American.*
Dana: *What?*
Robin: *What?*

Carrie: It's a long story. How's your host brother, Robin?
Robin: He has a girlfriend.
Dana: Bummer. :(
Robin: Her name is Brooke, and she's beautiful. :P

I laughed. Robin had just stuck out her tongue at me. I felt for her. I'd met her host brother while I was in London. Kit was really cute, and he had the nicest British accent.

Carrie: Dana, got any dates yet?

I groaned. I'd failed to mention my lapse of judgment when I e-mailed them yesterday. Carrie, of course, would ask. I debated what to tell them.

Dana: Not really. I'm going on an outing with Alex this afternoon.
Carrie: Alex Turner Johnson?
Robin: Thought he was boring.
Dana: He is. The purpose of our outing is to show him exactly how dull he is.
Carrie: Why bother?

Good question. Trust Carrie to get to the heart of the matter.

Carrie: Hello, Dana! Why aren't you answering? You don't like him, do you?
Dana: No way!

And I didn't like him. At least, not in the boy-girl kind of way that Carrie meant. My point system proved that Alex wasn't the one for me. I glanced at my watch. Yikes! Alex was going to be here at any minute.

I sat on the front steps that led into Renée's house. The houses on this street were all brick, very narrow in the front, and hemmed in by houses on either side. So different from my home back in Mustang, which had a relatively large yard and space between it and the other houses.

Renée's bike was leaning against the wall beside me. I'd thrown on a navy blue sweat suit because the weather was already cool in Paris. Pleasantly cool, but I figured it would be close to dark by the time we got back, and it would be much cooler then. I wore a baseball cap too.

I glared at the bicycle. I couldn't remember the last time I'd ridden a bike. I hoped that I remembered how.

I heard the whir of wheels, turned, and froze.

Alex brought his bicycle to a grinding halt only inches away from me. He wore an honest-to-gosh cyclist's outfit. The shorts and the jersey were hugging his body like a second skin. It looked like he'd probably had to melt down his body and pour it into those clothes to get them on. The muscles on his calves were well-defined—just like the muscles carved onto the marble statues I'd seen yesterday.

And his thighs looked rock hard—like granite. I swallowed.

"Don't you have a helmet?" he asked.

I snapped my gaze to his. Gosh. Even his shoulders looked firm. I remembered being surprised when I'd punched him yesterday. I was stunned. "You cycle for real, don't you?"

He removed his helmet. His brown hair was plastered to his head. "Yeah. As a matter of fact, we're going to cycle over one of the roads that Lance Armstrong rode when he won the Tour de France in 1999."

I had watched the Tour de France that year, amazed that a person who had recently conquered cancer had managed to win the most prestigious cycling race in the world. Lance Armstrong was an amazing individual. I would have gladly told Alex that I admired Armstrong if I weren't so upset with Alex.

"You told me that you didn't have time for sports," I reminded him indignantly.

"I said I didn't have time for *school* sports. Mustang doesn't have a cycling team," he remarked. He extended his helmet. "You can wear my helmet."

That action seemed a little too personal, and I definitely did not want to get personal with this guy. I backed up a step. "That's okay. I'll be fine."

"Dana, it's really dangerous to cycle without a helmet," he said seriously, like a parent lecturing a child.

51

"It's okay for you to be in danger but not me?" I shot back.

"This excursion was my idea. I'd feel bad if anything happened to you," he said quietly, as if he was embarrassed to admit it.

"I kinda like the idea of you feeling guilty," I said.

"And I prefer the idea of you not getting hurt. Let's switch headgear," he suggested.

If I were honest, I wasn't all that confident in my ability to keep the bike upright. I just hoped that before we were done, I wouldn't regret not having shin guards and elbow pads. I handed him my cap, took his helmet, and settled it into place.

He grinned, that lopsided, cute grin. "That's some stunning outfit."

"This isn't a date," I pointed out. But I wished that I had worn something a little nicer. I hadn't even bothered to freshen up my makeup. What was I thinking? What did I care? This guy was Alex Turner. American. Not French.

I watched while he shoved my cap into one of the pockets on the back of his jersey. Indignation ran through me. "Aren't you going to wear my cap?"

He shook his head slightly. "Pink really isn't my color."

"But it makes such a fashion statement," I exclaimed.

He blushed. "A fashion statement I can do without, thanks all the same. Come on. We've stalled long enough. Follow me," he ordered, and began pedaling.

I grabbed Renée's bicycle, hopped on, and started after him.

We cycled out of the city, alongside the lush green countryside. I was embarrassed because Alex had to keep slowing down so I could catch up to him. He'd even walked up a couple of hills with me, pushing his bike and mine. Of course, he'd only done that after he'd reached the top of the hill, glanced back, and realized I was fighting an uphill battle that I probably wasn't going to win. The guy was so totally in shape that I couldn't help but be impressed.

I remembered all the riders whizzing by during the broadcast of the Tour de France, and it was obvious to me that Alex was pretty durn close to being in their league.

By the time we arrived at the hilltop where he finally stopped, I was breathing hard, and my muscles were trembling.

He looked like he'd just taken a Sunday stroll.

"You took that curve back there awfully fast," I chastised as I took off the helmet.

He touched a little monitor on the handlebars of his bike. "Forty-two miles an hour."

"You are serious about this," I murmured.

"Actually, I'd like to ride in the Tour de France someday," he said as he took our bikes and leaned them against a tree.

I was still catching my breath. He removed

his backpack and took out a blanket, then spread the blanket over the ground. I slipped my backpack off my shoulders. I had my sketch pad and my pencil, but that was about it. I couldn't imagine trying to cycle while carrying anything else.

He glanced over his shoulder. "Sit down."

I dropped onto the blanket, grateful for the opportunity to rest my legs. Alex handed me a bottle of juice. Nothing had ever tasted sweeter as I squirted the liquid into my mouth. And it hit me that he'd put a lot of thought into this excursion—even though it wasn't a date.

"I've got some goat cheese here, some apples, a baguette, a few other things. Just help yourself," he offered as he spread out the snacks.

"You thought of everything," I murmured, breaking off a piece of the crusty bread and some cheese. To my great surprise, I was famished.

He gave me that lopsided grin. "I get hungry when I cycle."

I smiled back. "I can see why. You don't exactly do a leisurely ride."

His face burned red as if my observation embarrassed him.

"What do you think of the view?" he asked.

I looked past him, and the breath backed up in my lungs. It was the first moment I'd actually looked around to see where we were. "Oh my gosh."

From where we sat, I could see the Eiffel Tower, framed by trees and deep blue sky. "It's beautiful," I whispered in awe.

"Worth sketching?" he asked.

"Definitely," I responded without thinking. Then I shifted my gaze to him.

He looked so pleased with himself. He settled back against the tree and picked up his sketch pad. "Guess you could sketch a tree," he teased.

I took my sketch pad out of my backpack. "I could. But I won't."

"You're rare, Dana," he said quietly.

I snapped my gaze to his. My heart was pounding in my chest. I didn't like the way he was studying me. Too intently, intensely. "Rare?" I squeaked.

"A girl who admits when she's wrong." He gave me a cocky grin that broke the mood.

Thank goodness.

"I'm so seldom wrong that I don't have a problem admitting when I am," I responded haughtily.

He laughed then, a deep, booming laugh. It echoed between the trees, echoed around my heart. His laughter was a definite three. Warm and full of life. I wished that I hadn't realized that.

I turned my attention back to the Eiffel Tower. "We'd better get busy here. It'll be dark soon."

I started sketching like crazy. The sooner I finished, the sooner we'd leave. And the sooner I'd be out of the presence of Alex Turner.

I got confused whenever I was near him. He was

from Mustang. That fact, in and of itself, guaranteed that he would not be romantic.

And yet here I was on a hilltop outside of Paris, gazing at the Eiffel Tower, an unexpected picnic spread before me . . . and a helmet resting beside my thigh because he didn't want me to get hurt. Even though it meant exposing himself to the dangers of a head injury.

I knew guys from Mustang. Had dated one. Romance was foreign to them. Alex was a definite contradiction. I couldn't figure him out, and I kept telling myself that I didn't want to.

I drew lines and shaded and worked hard to concentrate on the drawing. Anything to stop me from noticing the guy sitting against the tree, sketching as well. I didn't want to notice the way his hand swept over the paper or the deep furrow in his brow.

Or the way the muscles beneath his jersey quivered. There should be a law against clothes that fit that snugly. They were too distracting.

An eternity seemed to pass before my sketch was complete. Relief coursed through me. This non-date that was closer to a date than anything I'd experienced with Todd was about to come to an end. I held up my creation for Alex to see. "What do you think?"

He grinned and took my pad. I watched him run a critical eye over the lines and shadows I'd drawn.

"Hey, this is really good," he said, his voice reflecting admiration.

My heart did a little somersault. It was the artist in me that longed for his approval, I told myself. Not the girl.

"Let me see yours," I prodded.

His face turned red, and he shook his head. He handed my pad back to me and closed his own. "Mine's not that great."

"Let me see," I insisted.

He shoved it into his backpack. "It's really amateurish."

"You have to expect that," I explained. "You haven't taken any art classes before."

He started to put away the remains of our picnic. I was really pleased with my sketch, but I felt bad that it had made him feel like his wasn't any good. "It takes lots of practice to draw well," I said kindly, encouragingly.

"I know." He moved closer as he gathered the last of the items and put them in his backpack.

I raised up on my knees, preparing to get off the blanket. My gaze fell on the horizon, and I stilled.

The majestic sunset cast a golden glow over Paris. I'd never seen anything so spectacular. Or so romantic. Picture-postcard perfection. I forgot to breathe.

I smiled warmly and turned to Alex. "Thank you for sharing this place with me," I said softly.

He was so close, his eyes so rich a brown, like

the most expensive chocolate imaginable. I felt like I was drowning in those eyes.

"Do you think a true artist could paint this view without imagining a couple kissing?" he asked quietly.

I slowly shook my head, captivated by his nearness. I couldn't remember Todd ever getting close to me and just hovering, waiting, creating an anticipation I couldn't explain.

Alex inched closer. "The kiss doesn't have to mean anything, but it should be there. Don't you think?"

I wasn't thinking at all. I was just immersed in his presence, the artistry of the moment. I nodded slightly.

He lowered his mouth to mine. His lips were soft and tender, not at all what I'd expected. Gentle, even. Todd had kissed like we were having a race, fast and hard, let's get to the finish line as quickly as we can so we can start over.

Alex kissed like there was no finish line, no rush.

If he gives this kind of kiss when it doesn't mean anything, I thought, *a real kiss from him . . . would be painted in colors so warm, deep, and vibrant that it would never be forgotten.*

Seven

Alex

I FLOPPED BACK on my bed in my small bedroom at Jacques's house. I stuffed my pillow beneath my head and glared at the ceiling. Kissing Dana had been a major mistake.

I couldn't figure out what had come over me. The artist in me had appreciated the view, the way the setting sun had cast a golden halo around her. . . .

But the male in me had been drawn to Dana as if there was no other girl on earth.

Stupid! Stupid! Stupid!

I'd been like a mosquito hovering just beyond a bug zapper, and then suddenly it's lured in and . . . zap! It's all over. In that one second everything changes.

The mosquito is burned to a crisp. I was a little more fortunate. But not by much.

Dana had definitely zapped me.

I jerked her pink hat off my head. I'd forgotten to give it back to her, and once I was safely hidden away in my room, I'd put it on. I couldn't explain why. It just made me feel close to her.

That closeness I definitely did not need.

Sitting up, I tossed the hat so it landed on the bedpost and did a little twirl. I grabbed my backpack from where I'd dropped it earlier at the end of the bed. I jerked open the zipper and pulled out my sketch pad. I shuffled through the pages until I found the sketch I'd drawn on the hilltop.

The lines were perfect, and not because I'd drawn them perfectly. They were perfect before I ever put them on paper.

The soft curve of Dana's mouth. The sweep of her thick, auburn lashes. The dozen freckles that dotted her nose and circled her cheeks.

Man, I'd never expected to think freckles were attractive, but on Dana they were like . . . highlights.

I knew that with art, it was often the smallest aspect of the work that made the difference. Details were important. Small details the most important.

So why was I becoming obsessed with little spots of brown that dusted the bridge of Dana's nose?

Because she had a cute nose.

And an adorable laugh. And eyes that sparkled constantly.

And a wonderful sense of humor. I couldn't remember when I'd last laughed. But when she had told me that she was so rarely wrong . . . Her comment wasn't that funny . . . but the way she'd said it as if she honestly believed it but understood that it wasn't true at the same time. I couldn't stop myself from bursting out laughing.

I had taken her to that hilltop to prove myself. From a particular vantage point, I could draw a captivating sketch of the Eiffel Tower. Instead I'd found myself enthralled with her.

To the extent that I had wanted to kiss her—desperately. I hadn't expected her lips to be so pliant. So warm. So welcoming. I'd become lost in her. Completely forgetting about my parents' divorce for the first time in weeks.

For the briefest of moments, I wasn't sad anymore. Or unhappy.

My life had been filled with all the colors on an artist's palette.

Whoa! These thoughts were definitely going beyond heavy. Dana was a girl from back home. The last one I wanted to kiss.

I did not want a relationship that involved feelings or a girl who managed to arouse fanciful thoughts. Dana was definitely not what I needed.

Relationships did not last, and I wasn't going to let a fun, smiling, artistic girl make me believe that they did.

Walking rapidly down the street, the cool evening air surrounding me, I knew the signs of panic. I'd felt them when my parents had told me that they were getting a divorce. My life as I'd known it until that moment sort of exploded like a supernova.

Leaving behind a black hole.

I felt like I was free-falling more deeply into that hole. All because I had kissed Dana—and more because she had kissed back. She had responded so sweetly. I needed to make sure that she understood that kiss on the hilltop—given to her during a moment of weakness or insanity or maybe both— meant absolutely nothing. *Rien*.

A sane person would have waited to talk to her at school the next day.

As a panicked person, I felt the need to talk to her that night, that moment, that very second.

She didn't live that far away, and it was close to eight o'clock when I knocked at her house. A woman who I assumed was her host mother opened the door. When I explained who I was, she invited me in, but I didn't want any witnesses to a possibly embarrassing situation.

Outside, I paced in front of the house while she went to get Dana. My heart was pounding like the bass drum in a band during a football-game half-time performance.

"Hey, what's up?" Dana asked as she stepped outside, closing the door behind her.

I halted in midstride. Man, she was cute. It was dark outside, but I could still see those freckles in my mind. *Forget the freckles,* I ordered myself. *Forget the feel of her mouth against yours.*

"I just wanted to make sure that you understood that kiss didn't mean anything," I announced.

She crossed her arms over her chest and leaned back against the closed door. I felt her eyes boring into me. Scrutinizing me.

"You explained that on the hill," she reminded me.

"That doesn't mean you understood what I was saying," I told her.

"I understood. The kiss meant nothing," she said softly.

I took a step closer. "I'm not interested in a relationship—not with you, not with anyone."

"That's good because I'm not interested in having a relationship with you," she blurted out.

I should have felt relieved. For some strange reason, I was disappointed.

"I plan to date a hundred girls while I'm in Paris," I said, striving to convince myself as much as her.

She uncrossed her arms. "I understand completely," she assured me. "My plan is to become involved with one guy—but a French guy. Not a mundane American." She took a step closer. "I want to be romanced by someone who invented the word. And the French did that."

"Good!" I snapped. "I'm glad to hear that."

"The kiss meant absolutely nothing to me," she reiterated.

Nothing? That's what I wanted, right? I wanted it to mean nothing.

"Excellent. So we can go on with our lives as if nothing happened on that hilltop," I told her.

"Absolutely," she stated.

I nodded, but my heart was thundering. I felt like an absolute fool as I turned on my heel and began walking home.

The kiss had meant nothing to her. I was apparently the only one affected by it. I couldn't figure out why I was so miserable.

Suddenly I was lonelier than I'd ever been in my entire life—and that was pretty dadgum lonely.

Private Internet Chat Room

Dana: Guys, I have a hypothetical question. Is it possible to enjoy kissing a guy that you don't like?

Robin: I've never kissed a guy, but I guess it might be possible if he was a good kisser.

Carrie: If you don't like him, then why is his mouth close enough to yours to even kiss?

Dana: I said it was hypothetical.

Carrie: Did Alex kiss you?

Dana: What are you, psychic?

Carrie: Oh my gosh. He did, didn't he?

Dana: It wasn't a real kiss.

Robin: Describe a false kiss.

Grrr. I wished I hadn't desperately needed help trying to understand what I'd felt on that hilltop.

Dana: Okay. So maybe it was a real kiss. But it didn't mean anything.

Carrie: But you liked it?

I took a deep breath. These were my two best friends. I could admit anything to them.

Dana: Yeah.

Robin: What are you going to do?

Dana: Try to forget it. He's completely wrong for me. He's not French; he's not romantic. And worse, he's from home. He is most definitely not my goal for this year in Paris.

Eight

Dana

I LOVED MY sketching class. Where else but Paris could I have three art classes, each one so incredibly different and yet each teaching me fundamentals that eased over into the other classes?

I'd received high marks for my Eiffel Tower sketch. I glanced across the room at Alex. I couldn't understand why he hadn't turned in his sketch. I wondered if he'd become self-conscious when I'd shown him my sketch on the hill—just before he kissed me.

Three days had passed, and I still couldn't get the memory of that kiss out of my mind. It was always there, haunting me. Whenever my art teachers swept their hands through the air and said to put more passion into my work, I thought of that kiss. Its warmth, its power. The sunset. It was so amazing the way everything had woven together like a perfect painting to create a lasting memory.

Yet all of it, particularly the kiss, had meant absolutely nothing to him. He probably didn't even remember the incredible sensations created by our mouths touching. He'd certainly rushed over to my house quickly enough that night to make sure that I understood the kiss meant nothing. That had hurt.

I knew it shouldn't have. I mean, he'd been upfront before he ever touched his mouth to mine. It was the artist demanding the kiss.

Not the guy.

And I was glad. I really was because the last thing I wanted was to fill this year with memories of kisses given to me by a guy from Mustang High.

I had to drag my attention away from Alex when the teacher started talking. It was getting easier to understand what my teachers were saying. I figured by the end of the year that I'd be much more fluent in French.

Madame Trudi explained that she was going to pair us up for a special project. She began calling out names. Girl, boy, girl, boy. I listened intently for my name.

"Dana! Alex!"

I groaned and slid my gaze to Alex. He had buried his head in his hands. I figured he was as thrilled as I was that we'd been paired together. When Madame Trudi finished calling out the names, she told us to sit by our partners. Why would she pair the two Americans?

I watched Alex reluctantly trudge across the room. The glower on his face was almost comical.

"Can you believe our rotten luck?" he asked in a low voice. "I was hoping she'd pair me up with Shari."

"I wanted Luc," I whispered back.

"We are going to move on to the human form," Madame Trudi explained in perfect French. "First the ladies will sketch the gentlemen, and then at the end of next week the gentlemen will sketch the ladies. Gentlemen, you will stand before your partners and remove your shirts."

My mouth dropped open, and Alex's eyes went as wide as two full moons.

"She's kidding, right?" he asked in a low voice.

I heard chairs scraping across the floor and girls giggling. "I don't think so." I smiled. "After all, this is Paris."

Alex slowly stood. He jerked off his *Gladiator* T-shirt, depicting Russell Crowe in full armor. In stunned fascination, I watched Alex's muscles ripple.

Wow! His cycling clothes had given me an idea of his shape, but seeing the actual hardened muscles was something else. This guy obviously worked out. Who would have thought a cyclist would look so powerful? An artistic cyclist at that. Alex was a contradiction to everything I believed.

And he wore such a cute blush. It started at his neck and went right up into his hair.

"Will you start sketching?" he ordered. "The sooner you finish, the sooner I can put my shirt back on."

"Oh yeah, right," I responded as I sat up straighter, put my feet on his chair, and set my notepad against my bent legs.

Like all the other girls in class, I took a quick glance around the room, comparing the models. I had definitely, much to my surprise, gotten the best. Even Luc didn't have muscles as defined as Alex's.

With Alex glaring at the far corner of the room, I settled back to slowly, ever so slowly, sketch that amazing torso.

"In a million years, I never would have guessed that Alex Turner had a great body," I told Renée as we wandered through a very chic clothing store.

I wanted something special to wear for my practice date. I'd purposely saved all my money from my after-school job back in Mustang so I could buy something in Paris.

Because who could come to Paris and not shop for clothes! This city had set the fashion trends for hundreds of years, and I absolutely could not come here without buying at least one designer dress.

"Maybe he is your destiny," Renée said.

I almost tripped over my feet. "What?"

"Fate keeps putting you together," she explained.

"No, teachers keep putting us together," I mumbled as I lifted a straight black dress off the rack. I imagined it with a colorful silk scarf tied at the waist.

"I think he's cute," Renée offered.

I wouldn't admit that in a thousand years. It somehow seemed a betrayal to myself. "He's okay," I muttered. "What do you think of this?" I asked, wishing I'd never started talking about Alex.

I didn't want to think about him. Tonight was a special night. My first real date with a Frenchie.

Renée angled her head. "With the right accessories, it could be perfect."

The right accessories ended up being a necklace that was a wide band of silver. It looked like something Cleopatra might wear. Little silver studs for my ears. A silver belt that looped around my waist and draped down one side. And silver shoes with three-inch spiked heels. Classy.

As I stared in the mirror, I thought I looked quite sophisticated. So what if the outfit took half my spending money? I hadn't even been in Paris a whole week yet. I'd have to be very frugal with my wardrobe money. My mom and dad were sending me a monthly allowance, but my wardrobe money was hard earned through my explaining to obese women why they didn't want to wear horizontal lines and to tall women why they didn't want to wear vertical lines. Some women had no fashion sense.

I turned slowly in front of the three-way mirror and wondered what Alex would think of the outfit.

I rolled my eyes. I could care less what he thought. I really could. Still . . . I wondered.

★   ★   ★

During dinner with my host family, I could hardly contain my anticipation about the evening. I was going on my first date with a French guy: François Morolt.

The name even sounded romantic. Although this was a practice date, I had hopes that it might prove to be more than that. My first week in Paris was nearing an end, and I didn't want to spend much more time looking for Mr. Romantic. Every week that passed was one week less that I'd have with him.

"How are you enjoying school?" Monsieur Trouvel asked.

"It's so different from Mustang," I enthused. "Especially the art classes."

"In what way?" Geneviève asked.

"Well, for one thing, I can't imagine any teacher back home telling the guys to take off their shirts," I explained.

"It's important for an artist to understand the human form," Madame Trouvel told me. "Someone once told me that da Vinci studied cadavers."

A chill went through me. "I'd rather use live subjects," I admitted. "Although I'm not sure how I'm going to gather up the courage to remove my shirt during the class."

Renée laughed. "French schools aren't that risqué. You'll be instructed to wear a bathing suit that day beneath your clothes."

Relief swamped me. "Am I ever glad to hear that!"

71

As soon as we were finished eating, Renée and I hurried upstairs to get ready for our dates. I really liked the way the black dress looked on me. It was a simple cut, but it hung perfectly over my short frame. It actually made me look a little taller.

I applied my makeup. Nothing too heavy. My main goal was to cover the irritating freckles. The Texas sun had a tendency to draw freckles on pale skin.

Not that it had ever drawn a freckle on Alex. He was so bronzed—

Stop that thought! I ordered.

I couldn't figure out why Alex tripped through my mind every five seconds.

I was about to go out on a date with a real French guy.

So why wasn't I excited? And why did I keep thinking about Alex, boring Alex, from Mustang High?

Nine

Alex

M Y HOST BROTHER, Jacques Reynard, and I were prowling the nightlife in Paris. It was way different from cruising in Mustang. The popular spots in Mustang were the Hamburger Hut, Giovanni's Pizzeria, and the bowling alley. Except on Friday nights. And then it was the stadium in the fall and the gym in the winter. Football and basketball. Spring and summer, it was the baseball fields.

Dances were limited to the homecoming dance and the prom.

In Mustang we didn't really have any hot spots unless beneath the stadium bleachers counted. I'd never taken a girl there. I don't know. It just seemed . . . really unromantic. And since I wasn't a romantic guy, I imagined girls rated it as less than unromantic.

Paris was filled with lights. Dazzling. No wonder it was known as the City of Light.

And Jacques knew all the places to go. Where kids our age tended to hang out.

With luck, tonight I would meet Miss Take My Mind Off My Troubles. A Parisian beauty who spoke a minimum of English.

We walked into a place that would be considered a nightclub in Mustang. But here it was more along the lines of a dance club. It looked like it catered to the under-twenty crowd. A live band had music bouncing off the walls while the band was bouncing over the stage. Laser lights beamed through the darkness.

Tables surrounded the dance floor. I didn't see any empty tables, and there wasn't a lot of elbowroom on the dance floor.

"We should have gotten here earlier," Jacques stated.

"I don't mind standing," I practically screamed in his ear.

Then I spotted three empty chairs. But the table wasn't empty. It was occupied by a lone girl. A very classy looking girl dressed in black. I tapped Jacques on the shoulder and pointed toward the table.

He nodded, which I took to mean it was okay to ask to share her table. I wasn't really up on French dating etiquette. Somehow that aspect of French culture had never come up in the French class I took back at Mustang High.

Avoiding the gyrating bodies of the dancers and the elbows of people sitting at tables, I headed to-

74

ward the lone girl and the three vacant chairs.

A few steps later I stopped short. Jacques rammed into me. I couldn't believe it. The girl was Dana.

She gazed longingly at the dance floor, her chin resting in the palm of her hand. If I'd been smart, I'd have turned around and head to the farthest corner of the room or, better yet, I would have beat a hasty retreat for the door. But apparently I had yet to unpack my intelligence.

I found myself striding to her table.

"What are you doing here?" I asked once I got close enough that a moderate shout would suffice in order to be heard.

She jerked back as if I'd woken her up. With disappointment reflected in her eyes, she pointed toward a guy on the dance floor, a guy dancing with two girls. "My date!" She leaned over and shouted above the loud music.

I couldn't help myself. I smiled broadly. "A very romantic guy!" I yelled back.

With a disgusted look she punched me playfully on the shoulder. I jabbed my finger over my shoulder. "This is my host brother, Jacques."

Without missing a beat or letting the introduction cool, Jacques took her hand and said, "Let's dance."

Dana looked the way a deer did when it began to cross the road and suddenly found itself staring into headlights. Her surprised expression quickly changed, though, and she looked pleased as Jacques led her to the dance floor.

I dropped onto a chair so we wouldn't lose the table. I was slightly annoyed that Jacques had asked her to dance before I got a chance. I guessed French guys worked fast. I also didn't like the way Jacques looked at Dana—with definite appreciation. Not that I could blame him. She resembled a model in that black dress. And she was wearing more makeup than I'd ever seen on that cute face of hers.

The makeup wasn't too heavy, but I'd noticed in the dim light that it covered her freckles. A shame since I liked those freckles.

The music finally stopped, and Jacques escorted her back to the table. I expected her date to return, but the guy was busy talking with another set of girls. Dana looked so forlorn.

When the music started up again, I grabbed her hand. "Come on."

She staggered after me. I stopped, stared at her, and suddenly realized why she looked like a model. She was wearing extremely high heels. They looked practically like stilts. "How can you walk in those things?" I asked.

"With a great deal of discomfort," she admitted.

I knelt down and slapped my thigh. "Come on. Let's take them off."

Her mouth gaped open. "I can't take off these shoes."

"Sure you can," I explained calmly, or would have if it weren't for the music. As it was, I was shouting calmly. "It's better than breaking your neck."

76

She put her foot on my thigh. I slipped the strap off her heel, the shoe off her foot. She had such tiny feet. I could see where the straps had cut across her arch. Unthinkingly, I rubbed her foot. It had to ache.

I stopped rubbing and glanced up at her. She was staring at me, her mouth slightly rounded. I figured I'd overstepped some unwritten dating code . . . like you can't touch a girl's foot unless she's your date or something.

"Other foot!" I yelled over the din of music and dancers.

She put her other foot on my thigh. I quickly removed the shoe and decided not to give this one the Turner treatment since she didn't seem too happy about it before. I stood and looked at the spiked heels. "Man, these could be used as weapons."

"But they're pretty, and they make my legs look pretty," she explained.

"Your legs looks pretty without them," I told her, and put the shoes on the table. Then I took her hand and led her to the dance floor.

The fast beat that had been playing suddenly dimmed into a slow song. I gave Dana an apologetic shrug, not certain if she would feel comfortable with our bodies pressing close after that kiss on the hilltop. "Go or stay?" I asked.

She hesitated for only one drumbeat before saying, "Stay."

Until she spoke, I didn't realize how badly I was

hoping that would be her choice. I drew Dana into my arms. I was unsettled by how perfectly she fit. It was as if the curve of my shoulder had been shaped for her face.

I was supposed to be searching for a French babe to spend the year with. Instead I was content to be exactly where I was for the moment. I wasn't thinking about my problems. I was concerned with hers.

How hard could it be to find a romantic guy in Paris?

The music drifted into silence. Dana stepped out of my embrace.

"Thanks," she said.

I shrugged. "Anytime."

We walked back to the table. Renée came over, a dark-haired guy in tow. She introduced him as her boyfriend, Jean-Claude.

"I'm so sorry," Renée announced. "I can't believe François is acting like a total idiot. Jean-Claude is very upset with him."

Dana waved her hand dismissively. "Don't worry about it. It was just a practice date."

Huh? Why in the world would Dana Madison need a practice date? She'd had a boyfriend in Mustang. Okay, so maybe Todd Haskell wasn't a good example. I couldn't remember ever actually seeing them in date mode.

"Want to leave?" I asked. "I'll take you home."

She smiled sadly. "I can't. I'm on a date."

"Do you really think François is going to notice?" I asked as kindly as I could.

She glanced at the dance floor, where François was gyrating like a scarecrow caught in the winds of a hurricane. "You're right. Let's go."

I grabbed her shoes and tapped Jacques on the shoulder. "I'm going to take Dana home. I'll catch up with you later."

I escorted Dana into the night. The lights of Paris surrounded us. We'd have to catch a bus to get home, but I hated taking her home when she looked so down.

"Let's walk along the Seine," I suggested.

Her eyes brightened briefly. "Okay."

"Do you want to put your shoes back on?" I asked.

She shook her head. "My hose will get ruined, but it feels too good to have them off. But I'll carry them."

"Nah, that's all right." I shoved one in each coat pocket.

"Don't forget to give them back to me," she commanded. "You still have my pink cap."

And it was still hanging on the post of my bed.

"I won't forget," I promised.

We strolled along the Right Bank, the north side of the river, known mostly for its dedication to art and the artistic. The river was beautiful. The lights from the Eiffel Tower, museums, and fantastic buildings reflected off it.

For reasons I couldn't explain, it hurt to see Dana disappointed in the evening. "François was a jerk," I announced.

79

She shrugged. "I know."

I couldn't believe the guy didn't realize what a great date he had tonight.

"Blind dates can be a bummer," I pointed out.

She gave me half a smile. "Tell me about it."

"Okay, since you asked, I will. A friend set me up with a girl this summer. She was a vegetarian. Not that there's anything wrong with being a vegetarian. But when I ordered a steak, she shrieked," I explained.

Her eyes widened. "You're kidding."

"No. Everyone in the restaurant turned to stare at us."

A real smile started to play at the corners of her mouth.

"Then when the food got there and I cut into my steak, she said I was cruel to animals," I told Dana.

Her mouth blossomed into a smile. I decided to exaggerate a little.

"When I began chewing my steak, she started crying and blubbering about the poor cow. How mean I was, how heartless. I didn't kill the cow. I was just eating it," I pointed out.

Dana started to laugh.

"The waiter had to bring an extra tablecloth over to dry her tears," I enthused, really getting into this tale of woe.

She laughed harder. Man, I liked her laugh.

"Did you stop eating the steak?" she asked.

"Are you kidding? I ordered another one."

She slapped my arm. "You did not."

"No, but I thought about it," I admitted.

"Did you ever see her again?" she asked.

"No, I just couldn't deal with the guilt. That night I dreamed that the ghosts of cows were haunting me," I teased.

She laughed until she had tears in her eyes. "Thanks, Alex," she said when she finally stopped laughing.

But it wasn't enough. Telling her a silly story about my vegetarian date. I didn't want her first date in Paris to be a bad memory.

I grabbed her hand. "Come on, let's take a *bateau mouche*."

We hurried along the bank of the Seine until we reached one of the pickup points for the *bateaux mouches*. I bought the tickets and we rushed onto the boat just before it pulled away from the dock.

Dana stood at the railing, gazing out on what I figured was the most romantic river in the world. I could certainly understand why she expected some French guy to sweep her off her feet. Paris had been built for romance. Even I could see that, and *romance* was a word that seldom strayed into my vocabulary. But I could see it all around us here.

Lovers strolled along the river in the moonlight. The horn of the boat sounded, an eerie echo that was romantic in its own way. We could see the Eiffel Tower, and I thought of Dana sitting on the hilltop with the sun setting over Paris.

And I thought of that kiss. I wasn't a novice when it came to kissing, but with Dana I'd felt like kissing her was all that mattered.

Definitely not what I wanted to be thinking about.

The breeze from the river was toying with her hair. I had a strong urge to play with it as well. Wrap a lock around my finger. My stomach was starting to knot up. I did not want to think of this girl as anyone important. She was just someone from home I was trying to be nice to.

But the lights of the city glistened off her hair, reflected in her eyes. I needed a distraction.

"I can't wait until you have to take your shirt off in art class," I announced, surprised by the huskiness in my voice. I'd intended the words to be a joke. Instead they'd ended up sounding like something I really couldn't wait for.

She slid that enticing green gaze my way. "I'll be wearing a bathing suit."

"No way!" I exclaimed. I feigned anger. "That's not fair. At least tell me that it's a two-piece."

Smiling sweetly, she shook her head. "One-piece."

"Man, how am I supposed to learn to draw the human form if I can't see most of it?" I inquired.

"Use your imagination," she challenged.

And that was my problem. I had way too much imagination. Heck, I already had her starring in my first full-length animated feature—and I wasn't even working for Pixar yet.

"Think I'll file a complaint with the school board," I muttered. "Unfair art practices."

She laughed softly. "Do they even have a school board here?"

I shrugged. "Who knows?"

She leaned over the railing and sighed wistfully. "I love this city."

I couldn't believe how much I wanted to kiss her again, but that one kiss had kept me up all night—no way could I make that mistake again. She was so sweet. So much sweeter than I wanted her to be. What would one more little kiss hurt? I leaned toward her.

"Somewhere out there, the most romantic guy in Paris is waiting for me," she murmured dreamily.

Reality came crashing back. Neither of us needed that kiss. She probably didn't even want it. Dana Madison wanted a French guy to fall in love with her this year.

And me? I didn't want anyone who might still be around when the year was over.

Private Internet Chat Room

Dana: My practice date was awful.

Carrie: What happened?

Dana: François was a party guy. Unfortunately, he wanted to party with everyone but me.

Robin: Sorry to hear that. I have a blind date tomorrow, and I'm not looking forward to it.

Dana: Hopefully it'll go better than mine did.

Robin: Kit set me up with one of his friends. The problem is . . . I wish my date was with Kit.

Dana: I understand completely. He is so hot, Robin.

Robin: Well, I'm sorry your night was a total bummer.

Dana: It wasn't a total bummer. Alex was there.

Carrie: What was he doing there?

Dana: He just showed up at the dance place with his host brother. He took me on a romantic boat ride along the Seine River.

Carrie: Romantic?

Dana: Very romantic.

I'd been unable to believe how romantic it had all been: with the lights reflecting off the river, him carrying my shoes, his nearness as I stood at the rail. I hesitated before confessing what would have made the moment perfect.

Dana: For a moment there, I thought he was going to kiss me again. And the worse thing is that I really wanted him to.

Ten

Dana

ON MONDAY MORNING I stared at the empty chair beside me in sculpting class. Where was Alex?

As my hands continued to shape the clay into what might pass, with a great deal of imagination, for a vase, I couldn't stop thinking about Alex. Or our romantic boat ride along the Seine River.

It had been incredible. He was fun to be with and had made me laugh. After he walked me home, I'd changed some of his scores on my rating chart. Not because I was considering him as a possible boyfriend. I definitely was not doing that. But since Renée had forced me to rate him to begin with, it seemed only fair to be honest about the scores.

I knew he'd hoped to meet a French girl at that dance club. Instead he'd sacrificed his night to make me feel better. I didn't want to think about how romantic that was.

Plus it made absolutely no sense.

Alex was from my hometown, for goodness sakes. He shouldn't have a romantic bone in his body, and yet whenever I found myself with him, as corny as it sounded, I thought of violins, starry nights, and dancing at midnight.

As much as I fought it, I enjoyed being with him. If I could just tone down my enjoyment so it resembled friendship instead of something more . . . I might be okay. I definitely did not want any romantic involvement with Alex Turner.

But I couldn't get him off my mind. It was as if someone had painted his portrait at the back of my brain. And of course, I had to see him with that cute, lopsided smile.

That image followed me from class to class. Worse—disappointment hit me every time I got to one of my art classes and discovered he wasn't there. Where was he? Why wasn't he in class? Had he dropped the art classes because he realized he had no talent?

As much as I hated to admit it, by the end of the day I was actually desperate to see him. Just to make sure he was okay.

I had just gotten my books out of my locker when I spotted Jacques, Alex's host brother, walking down the hallway. I called out to him. He immediately stopped, and I rushed over.

"Alex wasn't in any of my classes today," I announced.

He looked at me as if he expected me to say more. Honestly, sometimes guys can be so dense. "Do you know where he is?" I asked.

Jacques shrugged. "Alex gets up and rides his bicycle at five every morning. This morning he wasn't back before I left for school."

My heart pounded against my ribs as I thought about how fast Alex rode his bicycle. What if he'd lost control, tumbled down a hill? "Don't you think you should be worried?" I demanded.

Jacques glanced around as if he didn't know what to say. Finally he met my gaze. "He's a big boy. I'm sure he can take care of himself."

"But what if something happened to him?" I insisted. "What if he's hurt?"

"I think my parents would have called the school if there was a problem," he explained.

"But what if they didn't know? What if—"

He laughed loudly, his laughter echoing between the lockers. "Do you Americans always worry so much?" He angled his head slightly. "Or are you just worried about Alex?"

I stiffened. "I'm not worried about him. . . . I just . . ." Was worried about him. Not because I cared about him romantically or anything. I mean, we came from the same hometown. That forced an unwanted bond between us. I slung my backpack over my shoulder. "Just call me if he's not home when you get there," I ordered.

★   ★   ★

87

The problem with being artistic is that I can see things in such vivid colors. Blood is a bright red. Bruises are a deep purple. Scrapes look like they hurt.

I kept having these horrible visions of a wounded Alex calling out to me for help. While I was sitting at the table in the Trouvel home eating *pain au chocolat*. The flaky pastry with a chocolate bar nestled inside was a popular after-school snack.

Madame Trouvel and Renée were talking quietly beside me. Madame Trouvel always wanted to know how our day at school went. It was nice sitting here after a grueling day of studies. Normally it helped me unwind.

Today I felt like one of those springs in a mechanical toy that gets wound tighter and tighter and tighter. Then when it's released, it hops over the table like crazy until it finally topples off.

"Dana, what's wrong?" Madame Trouvel asked.

I jerked out of my dire thoughts and announced, "Alex wasn't at school today. Jacques doesn't know why he didn't go to school. I don't even think he knows where he is."

"Maybe you should call him," Madame Trouvel suggested.

I balked at that idea. "I don't want him to get the wrong impression."

"What wrong impression?" Renée asked. "That you care?"

"I don't care about him," I insisted while a little

88

voice in the back of my mind called me a liar. "I mean, I don't care about him personally, but he is my model, and if he's not in class, I can't complete my sketch project." The little voice in my head yelled that was another lie. I had memorized every line of his torso. I could draw him in my sleep. And that was a very disturbing thought.

"He is far from home with no one to call him," Madame Trouvel reminded me. "I think you should do it as a courtesy, one American to another."

Relief coursed through me. "Right," I acknowledged. "One American to another." Nothing personal. I would be like an ambassador of goodwill.

I excused myself from the table and hurried to my room. Sitting at my desk, I located Jacques's number in the school directory and quickly dialed it. My heart was hammering. Jacques answered, and I asked to talk to Alex. An eternity seemed to pass before Alex finally came to the phone.

"Why weren't you at school today?" I immediately demanded, hating the concern clearly reflected in my voice.

"I didn't feel like going to school today," he replied.

Didn't feel like it? "You mean, you didn't feel well?" I asked. "As in sick?"

"Sure," he responded, but there was a strangeness in his voice, an emptiness I'd never noticed before. "Look, I gotta go," he announced.

Before I could respond, he hung up abruptly. I

stared at the receiver. I had allowed *this* guy to fill my head with romantic notions? Had actually thought he might be romantic? Obviously I was becoming so desperate for romance that I was seeing it where it had no possibility of existing.

Two days later I was sitting on the steps outside Jacques's house. Alex still hadn't come to school. Jacques would only shrug when I asked him about Alex. Some host brother he was turning out to be. I'd rung the doorbell, but no one was home.

Naturally my creative mind imagined Alex being rushed to the emergency room with a burst appendix or something worse. But my rational mind insisted that I stay put. Sooner or later someone would come home, and I'd get to the bottom of Alex's disappearance.

I didn't care about him personally—I repeated that litany over and over. I did not care about him. But his absence was affecting my sketch project, and that I did care about.

My mouth dropped open when I saw a cyclist whizzing along the street. I recognized the outfit. Heck fire, I recognized the body. He didn't feel well enough to come to school, but he felt well enough to cycle? If I wasn't so angry, I would have been relieved.

Alex brought his bicycle to a skidding halt and removed his helmet. "What are you doing here?" he asked, clearly annoyed.

Incredulous, I slowly rose to my feet. "Don't you realize that they'll send you back home if you skip classes?"

He shrugged. "Let them send me home. It wasn't my idea to come here in the first place."

I couldn't believe his attitude. He seemed so different from the guy who had rescued me from the blind date on Saturday night. Had I done or said something to upset him? I stepped closer to him. "What's wrong?"

He started chaining his bicycle to the wrought-iron fence in front of the house. "Nothing."

"Nothing," I muttered. His attitude was really irritating. He made me feel like I was a pesky fly buzzing around his face. "Fine," I snapped. "If you don't want to talk about it, that's just fine with me. But I'm not going to fail my sketch class because you're suddenly homesick."

He bolted upright. "I'm not homesick!"

"Whatever," I said, with a wave of my hand. "I've got my sketch pad and a project to finish. You're taking off your shirt, buddy. Now!"

I couldn't believe that Alex had actually been cooperative. He'd invited me into his host family's home. We went to the den. It was a small room filled with bookshelves and a large fireplace. Right now, no fire blazed within the hearth, but I was way too warm anyway—just looking at Alex and that well-defined body of his. Mustang definitely needed a cycling team. I was actually considering heading a committee to push for one when I got home. Not that I wanted to win points with Alex. I had realized he was absolutely nonromantic.

He had removed his shirt. But he stood beside the hearth, glaring at a distant wall. Impatience shimmered off him like the noonday sun off hot asphalt.

Sitting on the couch, I remembered how he'd glared in class as well. The guy obviously didn't like to show off those amazing muscles. But there was something different about him this time.

I studied the portion of the sketch I'd done in class. I'd managed to do most of his face. I'd left off his mouth, hoping at some point before I was finished that he'd give me one of his lopsided grins. But I'd drawn in his eyes, shaded them . . . glaring eyes.

I glanced up at him, nearly taken aback by the difference in his eyes. Now I noticed what I hadn't before. His eyes contained a profound sadness. More than homesickness was involved here.

"What's wrong?" I blurted out.

He slid his gaze to me. "I don't want to do this stupid project."

I set my sketch pad aside and leaned forward, bracing my arms on my thighs. "I'm serious, Alex. Something is upsetting you."

"Will you just draw?" he demanded impatiently.

I honestly thought the guy was going to cry. I could see him swallowing repeatedly, and he was looking at every object in the room but me. A horrible thought occurred to me. "Is your host family abusing you?" I asked softly.

A corner of his mouth lifted in a sad sort of smile. "No, Dana, it's nothing like that."

But it was something. Without realizing it, he'd admitted *something* was wrong. "What is it, then?" I prodded gently. "Did someone die?"

"Not someone. Something. My parents' marriage died." He sank to the floor as if defeated. "My coming here was their idea. They thought it would be easier on me if I wasn't there while they went through the divorce proceedings—like it isn't my life that's being affected as well."

My heart went out to him. Although it had been years since my mom and dad had split up, I could still remember the raw edge of that pain. It lessened over time, but I wasn't sure if it would ever go away completely. Sometimes I even imagined that they'd get back together. My head knew it was an absolute impossibility . . . but my heart refused to believe.

I slid off the couch and sat beside Alex on the floor. "You seemed fine when we were together Saturday night. What happened?"

He sighed heavily. "My mom called on Sunday. She gave me my dad's new phone number. He's moved out, has his own place, and it just made the divorce more real. I can't bring myself to call my dad. It's strange. I don't have his number memorized. I have to look at a piece of paper to call my dad. Now you understand why I dropped his name for the time I'm here. I guess I'm pretty mad at him. At both of them, really."

I wanted to comfort Alex as I'd never wanted to comfort anyone. I took his hand, glad he didn't resist. His hand was so much larger than mine that I wasn't certain if my small hand could offer him much comfort. "When I was ten, my parents got divorced. The hardest part was realizing that their divorce wasn't my fault. I kept thinking if only I'd kept my room clean or been more polite or made better grades . . ."

He nodded slightly. "I keep thinking if I'd gotten involved in school sports or didn't spend so much time drawing, my parents might have stayed together. So many of the things I do, I do alone. Maybe if I'd involved my parents . . ."

I touched his cheek. "They fell out of love with each other, Alex. They didn't fall out of love with *you*. Nothing you did or didn't do caused their divorce to happen."

He took my hand from his cheek and laced our fingers together. He held my gaze, and I felt like I was swirling endlessly in those soulful brown eyes of his. I could actually see his pain, his frustration, and his doubts.

"What finally convinced you that it wasn't your fault?" he asked huskily.

"It wasn't any one thing," I explained. "Divorce is like death. You mourn, you hurt, and you start to heal. My parents are so much happier now. As difficult as it still is sometimes, I know it's a good thing that they didn't stay together."

"I'm a long way from feeling like this divorce is a good thing," he confided.

I squeezed his hands. "It was incredibly hard watching my dad pack up his things and carry the boxes out to a moving van. That tore me up inside. Maybe your parents are right. It'll be easier not seeing everything."

He shook his head. "No. When I left Mustang, I had a home and a family. When I get back, I'll have nothing."

Eleven

Alex

THE FOLLOWING MORNING Jacques and I were cycling just outside Paris. I really couldn't have asked for a better host brother. He'd told me that Dana had been asking about me at school, but he hadn't told her that I was in a "black" mood, as he called it. Jacques had left me to sulk, which was exactly what I thought I wanted.

Until Dana had shown up on the doorstep.

I started pedaling harder, feeling the burning in my calves and thighs that meant I was pushing myself. But I wanted to do more than push *myself*. I wanted to push away thoughts of my parents' divorce, but more, I wanted to push away thoughts of Dana.

Or more specifically, the attraction I was feeling toward her. It would have been incredibly easy yesterday afternoon to pull her into my arms and kiss her. I couldn't believe how badly I'd wanted to do just that. When she'd touched my cheek, I'd felt a jolt of electricity shock my system.

She was tender and gentle, with the sweetest smile and the kindest eyes. I hadn't meant to pour out my soul to her, but it had been the most natural thing I had ever experienced. She was kind and generous and really seemed to care.

"Slow down!" Jacques called after me.

But I couldn't. I was scared, scared like I'd never been scared. I hadn't been this frightened when my parents told me about the divorce. I was falling for Dana. Hard.

I knew that emotionally I was a wreck. The disintegration of my family had left me feeling hollow and empty. I needed something to fill that black hole. Dana was convenient but completely wrong. I needed a French girl. I had no intentions of hurting anyone, but with Dana, I would constantly worry that I might hurt her. Still, I liked her, and she seemed to like me. The way she'd looked into my eyes . . .

I slipped my water bottle out of its holder on my bike and squirted the water on my face. A little shock therapy to bring me back to reality. Dana wanted romance. Flowers, poetry, the whole nine yards. And she wanted a French guy. Heck, we were both only going to be here a year. We'd have no other time in our lives when we could get involved with a foreigner. It was this year or never. Frenchies for us both.

I slowed down, my heart hammering. I wasn't certain if it was thoughts of Dana causing that reaction or the way I'd barreled down the hill. Jacques caught up to me.

"Are you trying to outrace that cute American girl?" he asked.

"I don't know what you're talking about," I lied.

He laughed. "You can't get her out of your mind, and riding like a maniac won't help," he assured me.

"I have no interest in Dana. What I'm looking for is a French babe. I thought you were going to help me find one," I reminded him.

He began to peel a banana. When you cycle seriously, you learn to drink, eat, and water the flowers along the roadway without ever getting off your bike. Sports commentators often remarked on the lovely flowers that bloom along the Tour de France routes thanks to the many passing cyclists.

"Maybe I should date Dana," he suggested.

I almost lost my balance and tumbled off my cycle. Jacques was good-looking and nice. Intelligent. He had a sense of humor. Heck. He was probably even romantic. My mouth had suddenly gone dry, so I squirted water into it before I spoke. "Sure."

That sounded like I didn't care. Unfortunately, I did. More than I wanted to admit.

I glanced over at him. "But first you have to help me find a French girl."

He smiled. "A bunch of the kids from our

school are meeting at Euro Disney on Saturday. That would be a good place to start."

I'd been to Disney World in Orlando, but visiting the theme park in Paris would be great fun. "I'll be there," I promised.

And I vowed to find someone to make me forget all about my parents' divorce . . . and more, to make me forget all about Dana Madison.

Forgetting about Dana wasn't going to be easy. I finally returned to school on Friday. When I strolled into sculpting class, Dana's face lit up like the Christmas lights strung along Main Street in Mustang. I couldn't remember if anyone had ever looked so happy to see me.

And what made it worse was how glad I was to see her. Only two days had passed since our last meeting, but it felt like an eternity. These thoughts were exactly what I did not need—or want. I was spending way too much time thinking about her.

I dropped into the chair beside her. I tried to ignore her honeysuckle scent that reminded me so much of home.

"Decided you couldn't run from your troubles, huh?" she asked, her eyes twinkling.

I shook my head. "No, just wanted to see you in a bathing suit."

I laughed at the blush that crept from her chin to her hairline. It was such a deep red that it nearly obliterated her freckles.

But in sketching class I was the one who blushed when Dana removed her top. She wore a modest emerald green bathing suit. A halter style that tied around her neck and left her shoulders bare. Many of the French girls in class weren't nearly as demure. String-bikini tops were in abundance. Some were so skimpy that they were really nothing more than string.

Any normal American male would have appreciated all that this class offered in the way of bare skin. I figured that I was as normal as they came, but I couldn't take my eyes off Dana. She'd kept her jeans on because we were only supposed to sketch from the waist up. But I kept wishing we were on a beach somewhere so I could slather suntan lotion on her back and see her bare legs.

"All right, Turner, you've looked—now sketch," she commanded.

"It's not so easy being a model, is it?" I pointed out.

"Draw fast," she ordered.

I wanted to, just because she wanted me to. I really did. I didn't want her to feel uncomfortable any longer than necessary. But my hands wouldn't cooperate. They were shaking as I struggled to draw the slender lines and the dainty curves that made up her body.

It had been so easy to sketch her on the hilltop—but that was before I realized I was falling in love with her.

Twelve

Dana

EURO DISNEY! I couldn't believe I was at Euro Disney in Paris—a much better place than an art museum to meet guys.

A bunch of kids from my school were meeting at the entrance. I was waiting with Renée and Jean-Claude. Jean-Claude had apologized so many times for the guy he'd set me up with that it had become a joke. Still, I felt a little like a third wheel standing there with them. He'd offered to set me up with someone else, but I'd declined the generous offer. By being a "free" agent, I could check out all the guys, go on rides with different guys.

I realized it would be like going to the Tastes of Mustang—an annual event held back home where all the local restaurants have booths so everyone can taste their food. Only this event would be the Guys of Paris. I could have a sampling of conversation and time spent with several of them.

I recognized several kids from my classes when they arrived. Everyone was excited and in a good mood. This day was going to be great.

Even the arrival of Alex couldn't dampen my mood—although I wasn't real thrilled with how glad I was to see him. I'd been sweltering in class yesterday with his eyes focused on me as he drew my form for our sketch class.

My mouth grew dry as I watched him amble over. He was wearing jeans and a Buzz Lightyear sweatshirt. I was beginning to think his entire wardrobe consisted of shirts geared toward movies. He gave me that lopsided grin and leaned close.

"Checking out the Paris guys?" he asked in a low voice.

I smiled. "You bet. I'm sure Mr. Romance is here. What are your plans for the day?"

"I am definitely going to find my French dream girl," he assured me.

"Well, that shirt will definitely get you a *girl*," I teased. I'd worn jeans as well, but a denim shirt and a bright green vest completed my attire.

He glanced down. "You don't think Buzz is sexy?"

I burst out laughing. "Hardly."

"He's my hero. Besides, someday I'll be doing movies that star guys like this one," he explained.

I raised a brow. "Oh, really?"

"Computer-animated movies. That's my career

path." I could almost see his chest puffing out.

"I'm more of a purist," I explained. "I'm interested in true animation, not computer."

"Everything involves the computer these days," he pointed out.

"But it doesn't all begin with the computer," I insisted. "I'd like to get involved in animated movies that follow the old tradition . . . one drawing at a time."

He looked like I'd just blasted him with Buzz's stun gun.

"You're interested in making animated movies?" he asked.

"Why do you think I'm studying art? I'd love to work for Disney." It had been my dream since I'd first seen *The Little Mermaid*.

"Amazing," he murmured. "I want to work for Pixar."

"You're going to have to get over not wanting to show people your work," I told him.

He smiled. "You may be right."

They opened the gates at Main Street Station, the gateway into the theme park. People began to jostle each other, trying to get into Euro Disney. I was swept into the crowd and was being pushed forward. I glanced over my shoulder and yelled back at Alex, "Good luck with your search!"

Alex gave me a thumbs-up. Strange how I wished we hadn't gotten separated. And how I really wished he had no luck at all.

*   *   *

103

The kids from our school tended to travel together in clumps of a dozen or so. It made it convenient for getting to know people. While I stood in line for the Big Thunder Mountain ride, I spent a lot of time talking with Gérard. I'd barely noticed him in our literature class, and now I couldn't figure out why. He was cute and interesting to talk with. I thought it would be fun to ride the roller-coaster-type ride with him.

He shifted slightly, and I could see Alex standing in the line right in front of us. He was talking with a beautiful, dark-haired girl. And bestowing upon her that adorable grin of his.

Jealousy shot through me like a speeding roller coaster. For some strange reason, I wanted him to look at me, leave that girl's side, and go on this ride with me. I wasn't real fond of roller coasters—and even less fond of watching Alex flirt.

I gave myself a mental shake. I was not jealous. I most certainly was not.

"Dana?" Gérard asked.

I jerked my gaze to his. "What?"

"Where were you?" he asked.

I shook my head. "What do you mean?"

"You have not answered a single question I've asked in the last five minutes," he explained.

I felt the heat suffuse my face. "I'm sorry. I got distracted."

"Does this part of the park make you homesick? It is supposed to resemble the American West," he informed me.

I knew this area of the park had been inspired by the American West. I was a little of a Disney nut, admiring a man who encouraged people to follow their dreams. And my dream right now was to become involved with a French guy. I was blowing my chances because I couldn't keep my attention from wandering to an American guy. And thinking about his dream of finding a French girl.

"No, I'm not homesick," I assured him. I leaned close. "To be honest, roller coasters make me a little nervous. I don't mind the speed, but the drops—"

"I will protect you," he promised.

I smiled brightly. His words sounded so romantic. It finally came time for us to load into the train. Even though Alex had stood before us, because of the way they loaded the train, he was now sitting behind me. I was grateful. I didn't want to see him "protecting" that dark-haired beauty.

The train took off, swerved around a bend, and rattled up an incline. Then poor Gérard lost it. As we took the brief plummet, he screamed as if he were watching the shower scene in *Psycho*. He closed his eyes tightly and scooted down in the seat, his knuckles turning white as he gripped the bar across our laps.

I could have sworn I heard Alex laughing hysterically behind me.

When the ride ended, we clambered out of the train. Out of the corner of my eye I saw Alex take the hand of the girl who had ridden with him and help her out. Gérard left me to my own devices. He was so pale and sweaty, though, that I decided being a gentleman wasn't on his list of top priorities.

"Excuse-moi," Gérard said. "My breakfast is not going to stay put."

I watched him hurry away. So much for romance. But at least he'd been considerate enough to explain his hasty retreat.

Alex chuckled as he walked past me and said in a low voice, "Would love to see that guy on a real roller-coaster ride."

I couldn't stop myself from laughing. As far as roller coasters went, this one was really pretty tame. Maybe I'd have better luck at the next ride.

I just sorta followed the group from one ride to another, meeting a guy here and there but no one who really impressed me as Mr. Romantic. I was getting quite bummed out and thoroughly disappointed.

We finally arrived at the Pirates of the Caribbean, and as fate would have it, Alex ended up sitting beside me in the boat. I really didn't like the way my heart did a little dance against my ribs.

"Having fun?" he asked.

"How can anyone not have fun here?" I asked.

"It's magical, all right, whether it's in English or French," he admitted.

The boat left the dock, humming along. We watched robotic pirates plunder an eighteenth-century Spanish fortress in a crescendo of explosions. When we floated by a setting that included robotic women, I leaned toward Alex. "Maybe one of those is your French dream girl."

He laughed. "Any one of those robotic dolls comes closer to being what I want than anyone I've met today."

"What about the girl you were talking to at Thunder Mountain?" I inquired.

"The key words there are *talking to,*" he explained. "She speaks English. I want someone who only speaks French."

I was dumbfounded. I knew we both spoke French, but neither of us was exactly fluent. We could get by. "How can you develop a relationship with someone you can't communicate with?"

"That's just it," he stated. "I don't want a relationship. I just want a warm body and willing lips."

As the day progressed into night, I was aggravated with myself. I'd spent way too much time thinking about Alex. I thought it was sad that he just wanted a French girl with willing lips and no emotional ties. Although I had to admit that my stomach knotted up every time I thought about those willing lips.

Still, his attitude seemed incredibly cold. But was what he wanted that much different than what I was after? I wanted a French guy, someone to romance me. But I did expect to care for him and to love him a little. I knew that without some semblance of love, there could be no real romance.

This French guy would be my first real love. As sad as it was, and in spite of all the time I had given him, Todd didn't count. I had liked him, but I never really loved him. It hurt to admit that, but it was also liberating because I could admit that what I'd had with Todd wasn't love. So maybe I deserved the half-price box of Valentine candy.

No. Even if you only liked someone, you didn't skimp on treating her special.

With Todd, I had just wanted to have someone to go steady with. I was in love with the idea of being in love.

Just like now. I was in love with the idea of being in love with a romantic French guy.

Now Alex, durn his hide, was making me doubt my goal for the year. I was *not* going to be using a French guy. We'd be friends, have fun . . . and then I'd leave.

I was standing on a bridge, gazing at Sleeping Beauty's Castle or, as it was known in Paris, Château de la Belle au Bois Dormant.

"Excuse-moi?" a deep voice echoed near me.

I glanced over my shoulder. A tall guy with blond hair smiled at me. "Remember me?" he asked. "Philippe. We have history together."

I smiled at him. "I remember."

I'd spotted him on and off all day. Every time I saw him, he was watching me; then he'd look away as if embarrassed. I figured he was a little shy.

"I thought you were with the other American," he explained.

"Alex?" I asked.

He nodded.

"No, we're just friends," I assured him.

"I am so glad to hear that. I was hoping we could go out next Saturday," he informed me.

My first real invitation from a French guy! I couldn't wait to tell Alex. Whoa! I didn't need to be thinking of Alex at a moment like this. I smiled brightly. "I'd love to go out."

"Bon," he added in a low voice, took my hand, and stepped closer to me.

With a glorious burst of color and a deafening crack, the fireworks began filling the night sky. Philippe put his arm around my waist and drew me near as the crowd closed in for a better look.

I wanted to find Renée, to let Renée know that I'd had a successful day after all. Philippe appeared to be very romantic as he watched the fireworks, his gaze drifting to me from time to time as if I was more important than the night sky.

Suddenly I spotted Alex nearby. He wasn't watching the fireworks. He was apparently creating his own. He stood beneath a nearby tree, planting a doozy of a kiss on a girl with long, blond hair.

I turned away, staring unseeing at the sky, my chest tightening until it ached.

Why did it hurt to know that Alex had found the warm body and willing lips he'd been seeking?

Thirteen

Alex

MONIQUE HAD A mouth that just wouldn't quit—which was exactly what I'd expected of a French girl. Oddly, though, images of Dana's kiss kept flittering through my mind. And worse, I kept seeing her smile, hearing her laugh, listening for the softness of her voice.

I recognized that initially Monique wasn't taking my mind off everything that I wanted her to, but I figured in time . . .

We ended the kiss. She used the tip of her finger to rub her lipstick away from the corner of my mouth.

"Samedi?" she questioned.

Saturday. *"Oui,"* I responded. We'd already agreed to have a date before she planted that kiss on me. I figured next Saturday would be filled with kisses exactly like that one. She certainly wasn't shy. But she did have to catch a ride with friends tonight.

"Au revoir," she purred, wiggling her fingers at me.

"Good-bye," I responded. I watched her stroll away, her hips swaying in invitation. She glanced over her shoulder, and I think she was a little sorry that I hadn't followed her. I couldn't explain why I hadn't. I was catching the bus home, had no one waiting on me.

I heard the fireworks burst overhead and glanced toward the castle. And that's when I spotted Dana standing beside some tall, blond guy whose arm circled her waist. She'd obviously found Mr. Romantic.

I watched as the guy leaned down, kissed her cheek, and then walked away.

I couldn't imagine that Dana would think it was romantic for a guy to abandon her in the middle of a fireworks display. I didn't even think it was romantic. I thought about heading home. After all, my mission had been accomplished.

But I enjoyed watching the way the fireworks reflected off her hair more than the way they brightened the night sky. Why did she intrigue me so much? She was cute, sure, but not beautiful like Monique. And Dana was totally, completely wrong for me. For one thing, she would definitely be there at the end of the year, back in Mustang, dogging my heels, wanting declarations of love.

Heck, she wanted more than declarations of love. She wanted flowers, candy, and poetry.

Romance. A seven-letter word that I tried to keep out of my vocabulary. But it sure had begun popping up a lot since Dana Madison had walked into sculpting class that first day.

I couldn't deny that I was drawn to her—against everything that was rational and made sense. As if I had no control over my legs, I found myself walking over to her.

I leaned close enough to inhale her honeysuckle scent. "I met with success," I announced.

She didn't take her gaze from the fireworks. "I noticed you playing tonsil hockey."

She sounded seriously aggravated. Was she jealous? Why did that thought please me?

"Just for the record," I began, "Monique kissed *me.*" Then I wondered why I felt the need to explain. It irritated me that I did. It irritated me even more that I wanted to know about the guy who had kissed her cheek. "So, how did your day go?"

She turned to me then and smiled brightly. "Great! I've got a date for next Saturday."

"Congratulations," I said, but my voice didn't sound as enthusiastic as it should. And my chest felt hollow. "Was that your romantic guy who just walked off?"

"Yes. He had to head home."

A burst of fireworks filled the air. Someone bumped into me, and I bumped into Dana. My arms went around her, my hands grabbing the railing of the bridge. "Sorry, I'm kinda wedged in," I explained.

"That's okay," she said in a low voice. "It's almost over."

She glanced back toward the sky. I figured since she didn't mind, I might as well enjoy her nearness. I edged a little closer to get away from someone's elbow. The top of Dana's head came right below my chin. Her back was against my chest. I liked having her so close.

What I found really strange was that I enjoyed just standing here with her more than I enjoyed kissing Monique. That made no sense. From a guy's perspective, kissing a girl should always rank higher than just standing beside one.

I heard Dana sigh in wonder as the final burst of red, green, yellow, and blue fireworks torched the sky. I smiled simply because I knew she'd enjoyed the sight so much.

People started heading for the exits, but it was a while before I could move back enough to give her room to move away. When she turned, I was surprised to see a sheen of tears in her eyes. She released a self-conscious laugh.

"I'm a sap when it comes to fireworks," she explained.

Why wasn't I surprised? I just smiled. She had such an endearing way about her, wanted romance so badly. I wished the guy who had originally been standing with her on the bridge had stayed until the end. I was a pinch hitter who really didn't want to play the game of romance. No matter what I thought I was feeling.

I'd never known seven days could be an eternity. But that week passed so slowly as I anticipated my date with Monique.

Now, at long last, I was on my dream date with her. She was blond, tall, and extremely beautiful.

I'd even put aside my usual cartoon-and-movie attire. I was wearing khaki Dockers and a light blue shirt. I'd forgone the use of a tie. If it were Dana sitting across from me, I probably would have pulled out my Disney villain tie. I figured she would have appreciated it.

But Monique wasn't Dana.

And that was good. I kept telling myself that was good as the maître d' led us to a table by the window. I'd brought Monique to La Tour d'Argent. The Silver Tower. It was one of the most luxurious and expensive restaurants in Paris. I figured if I wasn't going to offer the girl love, I could at least treat her to a decent meal and a good time.

And money wasn't a problem. I suspected because of the guilt they harbored at sending me away, my parents had been very generous with spending money. "So you can have a year you'll never forget," they'd told me. But I figured they really wanted it to help me forget what was happening on the other side of the ocean.

Besides, I figured there was a chance Dana's date

might bring her here. Mr. Romance. Where better? And I would be able to see for myself that she was having a good time.

I shoved that thought aside. Tonight wasn't about Dana. It was about me and Monique and willing lips.

Monique wore a slinky blue dress that hugged her body like a second skin. I should have been impressed. Instead I kept thinking about a simple black dress that had held my attention one night. I kept thinking about Dana.

My thoughts were insane.

Monique smiled. Man, she had a gorgeous smile.

"Goofy!" she squealed, and laughed.

Nodding, I smiled back. Her English was limited to three words: Mickey Mouse and Goofy repeated in an adorable accent.

We'd discussed Mickey pretty much all the way to the restaurant. While waiting for our table, we'd begun the discussion of Goofy. It appeared she was ready to continue the discussion.

My knowledge of French wasn't so lame that I couldn't carry on a conversation with Monique. After all, I'd managed to communicate that I wanted to take her out and understood that she was interested in me.

But as the evening progressed, I realized that she laughed at everything I said in English. She didn't understand a word. She laughed when I spoke in French as well.

As the waiter brought our desserts, I realized that I hadn't thought about my parents' divorce in about . . . five minutes. And I had never expected to be so bored.

I had stupidly thought I would welcome the absence of conversation. . . . Instead I found myself looking forward to the end of the evening.

I knew that my feelings weren't fair to Monique. She was pretty and sweet.

But I couldn't tell if she was smart or interesting. Okay, I had to admit that I had learned a valuable lesson. I needed a French girl who could speak a little English.

Fourteen

Dana

R-*O*-*M*-*A*-*N*-*C*-*E*.
    I considered tattooing those letters across my forehead. Maybe then one of these guys would get the message.

I wouldn't classify my date with Philippe as awful. I was fairly certain that he was a wonderful conversationalist, but he spoke so little English that I couldn't be sure.

As we walked along the street toward my house, he kept pulling me close and telling me to listen to the language of the body. Unfortunately for him, my body was translating loud and clear—this guy was not the man of my dreams.

He'd taken me to a see a French film that contained no subtitles—and why should it? I was in Paris, for goodness' sake. But I just couldn't connect to the movie, so I sat there the whole time wondering how Alex's date was going. It was so totally uncool to be sitting in a darkened theater with one guy while thinking about another.

And then Philippe had pulled a Todd. Maybe it was even worse than a Todd. He'd taken me to McDonald's for dinner. Not that I don't normally like McDonald's. But in Paris? With a guy who I'm hoping is Mr. Romance?

The twin yellow arches just didn't set the mood that I wanted. I was more than ready for this date to end as I walked up the steps to my house. I turned to face Philippe.

"*Merci*," I said softly. "*Le soir*—the evening was wonderful."

He pulled me into his arms and planted his mouth on mine as if he intended to lay down roots. My first kiss from a French guy. I had expected to be swept off my feet. Instead my mind wandered to Alex, and I wondered if Alex had kissed his date good night.

I knew a person's mind really shouldn't wander during a romantic kiss. It sort of defeated the purpose.

Philippe slipped his hands beneath the hem of my shirt. I felt his palms on my bare waist. I grabbed his wrists and jerked back. "*Non, non, non.*"

I laughed, trying to make light of the uncomfortable situation. I'm not a prude, but I didn't expect a guy to touch me intimately until I was ready for the intimacy. And it took a lot more than a movie and fries to achieve that goal. It took hearts as one and souls calling out to souls.

Philippe drew me back against him and whispered near my ear, "You are not listening to the language of the body."

I squirmed, trying to extricate myself from a place I definitely did not want to be. Panic began to settle in. I figured if he wouldn't get the message, I could scream. The Trouvels were home and would be certain to hear me.

Suddenly Philippe staggered backward, and I saw Alex standing there. His hand was gripping Philippe's shoulder, and I realized he'd pulled him back.

"She said no, and no in English or French is no," Alex declared in a tight voice.

I had this flash of a notion—I knew how damsels in distress had felt when the knight in shining armor saved them from the dragons.

"Americans!" Philippe spat as he jerked free of Alex's hold and walked away in a huff.

I looked at Alex. Maybe his armor was a bit tarnished, but I was still appreciative that he'd stepped in when he did. "Thanks."

He shrugged. "You okay?"

"Yes. I don't think he meant any harm. He was just a tad more enthusiastic than I wanted him to be." I furrowed my brow. "What are you doing here anyway?"

"I was just walking home after my date with Monique," he explained.

Ah, yes, Monique. I couldn't imagine her saying

no to a kiss from Alex. I was taken aback by the jealous pang that hit me, and I was determined to ignore it. Or at least make Alex think that I didn't care. I forced myself to ask lightly, "So, how did it go?"

"It went great." A corner of his mouth lifted, and he shook his head. "It was awful."

"I'm sorry to hear that," I said, although I felt like jumping with joy. What was wrong with me? "What happened?"

He shoved his hands into his pockets. "The only English word she kept repeating was *Goofy*. About halfway through the meal, I realize she thought that Goofy was my name."

I couldn't help myself. I burst out laughing—not so much because I thought it was funny. But because I was incredibly relieved. "You're kidding me, right?"

"I wish. She was sweet, but I don't think she was the brightest bunny in the burrow. Hard to tell, though, since she didn't speak English and my French is only passable," he explained.

Passable enough to get a date, I thought. *But not enough to enjoy the date.* I thought about Philippe's suggestion to listen to the language of the body. I was incredibly glad that Alex hadn't known about that advice.

I must have thought about him a hundred times while I was on my date—and that was so unfair to Philippe. How could any evening hold the magic of romance if I was thinking about another guy?

Alex jabbed his thumb over his shoulder. "Hey, just so this evening isn't a total waste, you want to grab something sweet to eat? There's a late night pastry shop around the corner."

The offer was tempting, and not just because of my love for chocolate. Alex looked terrific. He wore khaki pants and a light blue shirt beneath a dark brown jacket. I wouldn't have been surprised if he pulled a tie out of one of his pockets. It looked like he'd put as much thought into getting ready for his date as I had into getting ready for mine.

Yet, we'd both had a bummer evening. I put my hand on my stomach. "Yeah, I think these McDonald's fries could use some company."

His mouth dropped open. "Tell me that your date did not take you to McDonald's."

I grimaced. "Afraid so."

He took my hand. It seemed so natural that I wasn't even sure he realized that he'd done it.

"I always figured the French were romantic," he murmured as we began walking along the dimly lit street.

"Me too. I had visions of flowers, candlelight, and poetry; French words whispered in my ear," I confessed.

He glanced over at me. A corner of his mouth lifted. "Maybe you expect too much."

I shook my head. "But this is the city of romance, Alex. I'll only be here a year. I have to pack enough romance into this year to last me a lifetime."

121

"Don't you think any guys from Mustang know anything about romance?" he asked thoughtfully.

I raised a brow. "Honestly? No. At least not the kind of intense romance that I want. I want to feel like the guy can't live without me, that I'm the center of his universe."

"Sounds like you're looking for some serious love," he mused.

"All I want is the romance," I assured him. Serious love would mean heartache at the end of the year, and I definitely did not want that.

"Do you honestly believe you can have one without the other?" he asked.

"Sure," I replied confidently, although I really was no longer certain. Was that where things were going wrong? I thought I could have romance without a long-term commitment?

We stopped walking, and Alex shoved open the door to a bakery. The aroma of freshly baked bread and pastries teased my nostrils. He waited for me to walk in first. Then he followed me to the counter. I looked through the glass at the assortment of pastries. "Any one of these is going to go a long way toward helping me to forget about my quest for romance," I admitted.

I ordered a chocolate-coated éclair while Alex ordered *chausson aux pommes,* a pastry filled with apples. We both ordered large milks. At the cash register I reached for my purse, a thin strap anchoring it over my shoulder.

"My treat," Alex announced, without looking at me. I watched him dig the francs out of his wallet.

I considered arguing. After all, we weren't on a date, but I didn't want to chance ruining the rapport we'd established. Besides, how many people in Paris could understand why I was searching so badly for romance? Renée didn't understand because she could not comprehend how totally unromantic the guys were in Mustang.

Alex knew the guys. He knew that in Mustang, I would never find the romance that I craved. It was just inconceivable.

We settled into a corner booth. Beside us the large window looked out on the street. It was after ten o'clock, but lovers strolled by, arm in arm. I could tell some were whispering, probably words of love.

With a sigh I took my fork and cut off a bit of éclair. I closed my mouth around the rich filling, the creamy chocolate, and the flaky pastry. I moaned softly. "This definitely hits the spot."

Alex chuckled. I watched as he dug into his pastry.

"I can't resist the lure of bakeries," he confessed.

"We have a bakery in Mustang," I chided.

He narrowed his eyes at me. "Donuts 2B8 is not a bakery."

He was so right. Three varieties of doughnuts hardly compared with the delicious éclair that was now making my mouth water.

"I'll probably go home a hundred pounds heavier," he murmured.

"Not the way that you ride your bike," I teased.

He smiled. "True."

His gaze held mine, and it occurred to me that I knew more about Alex Turner than I knew about any other guy in existence—certainly more than I knew about Todd. I knew Alex's dreams: to cycle in the Tour de France, to work for Pixar. I knew all the self-doubts he was experiencing over his parents' divorce. I relished the sound of his laugher and loved that lopsided grin.

Loved? How could I love anything even remotely related to a guy from Mustang?

I quickly dropped my gaze to his plate. And there were those amazing hands of his resting on either side of it. Originally, hands weren't on my guy score sheet, but after watching him day after day in sculpting class shaping the clay . . . Well, I'd had to add it to my list of things about a guy to consider. And I'd given him a three.

"You can have some if you want," he offered quietly.

I jerked my eyes back to his. "What?"

"You're staring at my pastry. Thought you might want to give it a try," he explained.

"Sure," I stammered, or would have if I'd had to say more than one word.

I watched him jab his fork into a piece of the pastry that he'd already worked free. Holding the fork, he carried the pastry to my mouth.

Sharing our food seemed so incredibly intimate.

124

My stomach knotted up, and I wasn't certain how I was going to be able to swallow. My heart was pounding as I closed my mouth around his fork.

He slid the fork out of my mouth and grinned. "Well?"

The apple-filled pastry was delicious. "Yummy. Want to try the éclair?"

"Yeah, I would. I'm a sucker for chocolate, but apples are healthier."

I laughed. "Right. And I eat carrot cake for the vegetables," I teased.

"Really? Me too."

We both laughed, and it was such a memorable moment. I'd never laughed with a guy. It was like a meeting of souls or something.

I cut off a piece of éclair, hooked it with my fork, and extended it toward him. He hesitated, and I wondered if he suddenly realized—as I had earlier—how personal it was to share food. I watched him take my offering, chew, and swallow.

"That's good," he agreed.

I was actually enjoying the evening. The disaster of my earlier date was a fading memory. But I was spending way too much time thinking of Alex in a romantic context. I needed to bring us both back to earth.

"Did you ever call your dad?" I asked.

All the sparkle went out of his eyes, and he shoved his pastry aside. "No."

I wished I'd kept my mouth shut. I hated seeing him looking so incredibly miserable.

I glanced at my watch. Midnight. I set my éclair aside.

"Why don't you call your dad now?" I suggested. "I saw a pay phone around the corner, and it's only five in the afternoon in Mustang."

He shook his head. "I can't, Dana. I've thought about calling him a hundred times this week, but it just makes the divorce too real, and I guess I'm not ready to face it."

I reached across the table and wrapped my hands around his balled fists. I could feel so much tension in him. "You know, Alex, it's already very real for your dad."

"Are you saying that's my fault?" he demanded.

"No," I replied softly. "I just remember when my dad moved out that I was afraid he'd stop loving me because he didn't live with me anymore. Later my dad told me that he had been afraid *I'd* stop loving him. If you don't call your dad, he might think that you don't love him anymore."

"I hadn't thought of it like that," he said quietly.

"He's probably just as scared as you are," I continued.

"I don't see how he could be," he snapped. "After all, it's *my* world that's falling apart."

"And his isn't?" I prodded gently.

Alex looked like I'd just dumped a bucket of cold water on him.

"You know, Dana, I hadn't really thought about what he must be feeling." He moved one of his hands out from beneath mine and combed his fin-

126

gers through his hair. "I've been so selfish."

I squeezed his hand. "You've been confused—and that's natural," I assured him.

"My dad's alone, just like me," he pointed out.

I jerked upright. "And what am I? A figment of your imagination?"

His face broke into a warm grin. "No, you're a very special girl."

He reached into his back pocket, pulled out his wallet, and dug out a scrap of paper. Then he met my gaze. "How do I say I want to make a collect call?"

"Let me look in my trusty pocket-size English-French dictionary." I pulled it out of my purse, riffled through the pages, then smiled triumphantly as I found the expression. *"Je voudrais faire une communication avec PCV."* I looked at Alex. "You need anything else?"

"You," he answered quietly.

My heart slammed against my ribs. I was certain that all the blood had drained from my face.

"Will you stay with me while I call him?" he pleaded.

I nodded, surprised by the warmth that flowed through me because he wanted me. My heartbeat returned to normal, but I knew that I'd never forget the way he looked at me after I nodded. Like I placed the stars in the sky.

The pay phone was anchored to a wall, not enclosed in a booth. Fortunately the street was quiet this time of night. I watched Alex drop some coins into the slot. I heard him mumble in French. Then he gave a deep sigh.

"The phone's ringing," he muttered in a shaky voice.

I moved closer and rubbed his back. He was so incredibly tense. He glanced at me, and I could see the apprehension in his eyes. Maybe this wasn't such a good idea. I was on the verge of telling him to hang up when he said, "Dad?"

I felt the tension between his shoulders increase. Then he released a strangled laugh. "Nothing's wrong. I just wanted to talk to you."

He turned slightly, and his voice became muffled, so I couldn't hear what he was saying to his dad. I continued to rub his back. Little by little, I could feel the tension easing away.

I heard thunder. A raindrop plopped on my nose. I glanced up. Even though it was night, the sky looked darker than it should. Another drop.

Lightning zigzagged across the sky. Thunder rumbled. And then a gush of water drenched me unexpectedly. I shrieked as the rain began to fall harder and harder.

Alex turned around. He was grinning broadly. "I gotta go, Dad," he said. "Me too."

He hung up and took off his jacket. He draped it over my head. Laughing, he ordered, "Come on, let's get you home."

I couldn't believe how quickly it had started to pour. We rushed down the street, our pounding feet causing the water to splash our legs. Just as suddenly the rain let up slightly but continued to fall.

We reached my house, and I hurried up the steps. I turned to face Alex.

His hair was plastered to his head. Drops of rain were rolling down his face. His clothes were soaked. Not that I was in much better condition.

"A lot of good my jacket did," he announced.

"It's the thought that counts," I admitted. He'd at least tried to shelter me. As the rain continued to bounce off him, I couldn't believe how thoughtful he was.

"Thanks, Dana," he said quietly. "Thanks for talking me into calling my dad. He was really glad to hear from me. He thought I was angry with him. Maybe I was, a little. I'm not so much now."

"I've been there, Alex," I explained. "It's hard, but you'll make it through this divorce thing okay. Trust me."

"I do," he said solemnly. His gaze darkened as it held mine. He dropped his jacket to my shoulders so he no longer had to hold it.

The rain began to patter gently against my cheeks. Alex cradled my face between his hands, tilted my face up slightly, and lowered his mouth to mine.

The night air was cool, the rain cold, and his mouth so warm. I stepped closer to him and twined my arms around his neck.

He deepened the kiss in that slow, unhurried way of his. My body grew so incredibly warm that the rain no longer mattered.

All that mattered was Alex.

Fifteen

Alex

DANA WAS INCREDIBLE. She was so giving.

I felt like she was pouring her soul into our kiss, pouring herself into me.

All the loneliness I had been feeling was melting away like a chocolate bar left out in the August sun.

Yet this was all so totally wrong.

I knew what I had to do. End the kiss now before she got the wrong impression. Before she realized that she was all I could think about.

Our lips parted. But my will was weak. I kissed one corner of her mouth. Then the other. Then the tip of her nose, where all her cute freckles were.

Then I drew back and met her stunned gaze. Her mouth was still open slightly, and I was tempted to again cover it with mine. Instead I forced myself to back up a step.

"Sorry," I muttered.

"Sorry?" she repeated, clearly dazed.

"Don't read anything into the kiss, Dana. It was just another one of those artistic moments. . . ." My voice trailed off. I couldn't complete the lie.

"Artistic moment?" she reiterated.

"Yeah, you know. Like on the hilltop. Only this was night. Rain. I could see the canvas, and it was just begging for a couple kissing." I usually wasn't a babbler. I just didn't want to hurt Dana. If she knew how much I was coming to care for her, she might feel the need to reciprocate. I didn't want her to put aside her dream of being with Mr. Romance this year.

But I also didn't want her to think that I was taking advantage—kissing her when I really had no right.

She nodded briskly. "I see." She removed my jacket from around her shoulders and extended it toward me. "Thanks for sheltering me from the storm."

She sounded so formal. I was really afraid I'd hurt her. I could only hope it was a small hurt, something that would go away quickly. If I told her what I really felt, I could risk taking away her dream. That thought sounded so egotistical. Like she would set aside her dream for me.

Maybe it was me that I was afraid would get hurt. Dana had never hinted that I meant anything more than a friend—unless I counted that kiss. It had gone way beyond friendship.

Yet she'd made it perfectly clear what she wanted this year in Paris—a guy willing to fulfill her romantic expectations. Other than "Roses Are Red," I really didn't know any poetry to recite. Knowing Dana, she was looking for a Shakespearean sonnet.

I took the drenched jacket. It really hadn't done a lot of good. She looked like a drowned kitten. An adorable drowned kitten. Man, did I want to kiss her again.

I backed up another step. The rain was still falling, but softly now. "See you at school," I announced.

"Yeah," she replied, sounding somewhat sad. "See you at school."

"About that kiss—"

She held up a hand to stop me from saying anything else. "I know. It meant nothing."

Turning, she opened the door. I watched her disappear into the house.

No, I thought with a sigh, *that kiss meant everything.*

Sixteen

Dana

ON MONDAY AFTERNOON I sat on the bed in my room, my legs folded beneath me. In the center of the bed was a flat package. Gift wrapped. The bow on top was crumpled. Like a cotton shirt that needed to be ironed. It looked like someone had used the bow over and over.

That someone was Alex.

I wondered if he'd wrapped the gift, changed his mind, unwrapped it, changed his mind, and wrapped it back up again.

I'd been so nervous about seeing him in our first class this morning. After that earth-shattering kiss that had meant absolutely nothing to him . . . I had seriously considered changing all my art classes. I just didn't know how I could face him again.

The moment I saw him in the hall, right before

our first class, my heart sped up. Then he spotted me, and I had difficulty breathing. My lips tingled as if they remembered that kiss we'd shared in the rain. A kiss I knew I'd never forget even if I lived to be a hundred.

It had been the most romantic moment of my life. Standing there with the rain falling on us, the warmth of our embrace, the heat of our mouths.

I stood in the hallway like a deer caught in head-lights as Alex walked toward me. A corner of his mouth lifted, but his lopsided grin looked sad.

"How are you doing?" he asked once he got close enough that he wouldn't have to shout.

I took a deep breath and lifted my gaze from that incredible mouth of his to his soulful eyes. "Great. I woke up this morning knowing that Mr. Romance was going to walk into my life today."

"I really hope he does, Dana. You deserve your dreams." He extended a flat package toward me. "Open this at home."

"What is it?" I asked.

His grin grew. "If I wanted you to know right away, I wouldn't have wrapped it."

"Why can't I open it now?" I insisted.

"Because I asked you not to."

And that was that. The gift had haunted me all day. I figured it was a silk scarf because the box was so flat. Although I couldn't imagine why he'd give me a fashion accessory. Actually, I couldn't deter-mine why he'd give me anything at all.

But here I was, staring at the thin box, wondering if I really wanted to break the spell it had cast over me. As long as I had the package, my thoughts drifted to Alex.

Who was I kidding? With or without the package, I'd be thinking of Alex.

I reached for the box, carefully removed the wrinkled bow, peeled back the wrapping paper, and lifted the lid.

I stilled. My breath backed up in my lungs. I could not believe it.

I was looking at a sketch. A sketch of me, standing on a bridge with Sleeping Beauty's Castle in the background. Fireworks filled the sky over my head. But it was my image that held me captivated.

I've never considered myself plain, but neither did I think I was any great beauty. But in this sketch, I looked . . . beautiful. Incredibly happy. Magical.

I stared in stunned disbelief at the signature scrawled in the corner.

Alex Turner
September 2000

Alex had drawn this? I'd never been more confused in my life. His attention to detail was amazing. He even drew my freckles. Why hadn't he turned in his sketch of the Eiffel Tower that he'd created that day on the hilltop? It certainly wasn't because my drawing had intimidated him. He was far more talented than I was.

I lifted the sketch from the box, and beneath was a scrawled note that read, *Thanks for Saturday night.*

What did that mean? Was he thanking me for

A. Going to the bakery with him?

B. Talking him into calling his dad?

C. Staying with him while he talked to his dad?

D. Kissing him as if I had a serious crush on him?

I shook my head. B. I could hear Regis asking if that was my final answer. Without a doubt. My presence didn't seem to mean much to Alex whether it was at a bakery or a pay phone. And as for the kiss . . . I didn't want to think about how much it hurt that it meant nothing.

Reaching across my bed, I grabbed the phone off the nightstand. With a deep breath, I dialed Alex's number. His host mom answered and promptly went to fetch him.

"Hello?" His voice was so deep.

"Alex, it's Dana," I announced.

"What's wrong?" he asked, and I could hear the concern in his voice.

"Nothing," I assured him. I glanced at the sketch. "I just . . . I just opened your gift. It's wonderful."

"It's no big deal. Since the rain from Saturday night continued into Sunday, I couldn't cycle, so it was something to do," he explained.

Something to do? With the details, it must have taken hours.

"I plan to have it framed once I get home. It'll be a great souvenir." I didn't know how to tell him exactly how touched I was by his gesture. I might even send it to my mom so she could see how I was adjusting to life in Paris.

"I'm glad you like it. Listen, there's someone here who wants to talk with you. I'll see you at school."

With that, he was gone.

"Dana?" asked a deeper voice with an incredible French accent. "It's Jacques."

Alex's host brother. "Hey, Jacques."

"I was wondering if you'd like to go out Saturday night?" I heard him grunt. "With me. Go out with me. On a date. A romantic date."

He seemed so nervous that it was actually cute. "I'd love to."

"She'd love to," I heard him whisper. Alex mumbled something.

"Wonderful," Jacques muttered. "I shall count the hours."

After I hung up, I sat there, staring at the sketch. Disappointment slammed into me. I had felt such an incredible bond with Alex on Saturday night that I had hoped he might ask me out. I had sorta hoped that the sketch was—a prelude to a date.

Sure, he wasn't French, but I was suddenly beginning to realize that where a person was from wasn't as important as the person.

Private Internet Chat Room

Dana: Well, guys, I have a date with a Frenchie. A really nice one at that, who is totally hot.

Robin: How did that come about?

Dana: Alex. He set me up with his host brother.

Carrie: Alex again? You can't seem to get rid of the guy.

The problem was, I realized that I didn't want to.

Dana: Enough about me. What's happening with y'all? Carrie, did you get things worked out with Antonio?

Carrie: No, it's such a mess. I've really fallen hard for the guy, and he cares about me. But that will end the minute I tell him I'm an American. :(

Robin: You might be surprised. I finally revealed my true self to Kit.

Dana: And?

Robin: :)

Dana: What does that smile mean?

Robin: He's not only my host brother . . . he's now my boyfriend!

Carrie: Way to go, Robin!

Dana: I knew that would happen once you stopped trying to hide your true self.

I was so totally happy for Robin. If only Carrie could resolve the situation with Antonio . . . and if only I could figure out what it was I really wanted this year while I was in Paris.

Seventeen

Dana

LATE SATURDAY MORNING, I was in the kitchen with Madame Trouvel, Renée, and Geneviève. We were preparing lunch in their small kitchen. Madame Trouvel was teaching me how to fix crepes, which are like pancakes—and are delicious. I figured that by the time my year in Paris was over, I would be a gourmet chef. I was already planning on cooking one meal for my family.

Like just about everything in France, cooking was an art. I loved watching Madame Trouvel move fluidly through the kitchen. With her dark hair and blue eyes, she reminded me of a graceful dancer.

The doorbell rang.

"I'll get it," Renée said, and headed out.

With a wide spatula I gently lifted my crepe off

139

the pan and placed it on my plate. I leaned low and sniffed. "That smells so good."

"You are a natural, Dana," Madame Trouvel stated.

I felt myself blush. "*Merci,* but you did most of the work. I just sorta followed along and did whatever you told me to do."

She laughed. "That is more than my daughters can often do."

"Oh, Maman," Geneviève whined. "That's not true."

Madame Trouvel leaned down and kissed Geneviève's cheek. "Sometimes, *ma chère.*"

Renée came back into the kitchen. She was holding a huge crystal vase filled with a dozen red roses and an assortment of tiny white flowers—baby's breath.

"Wow!" I enthused. "Those are beautiful."

She smiled brightly. "They're for you."

I felt like someone had knocked the breath right out of me. "For me?"

"Oui." She set them on the counter, removed the card, and handed it to me.

My hand was actually shaking as I opened the card. It simply said, *Jusqu'à ce soir.* Until this evening.

I pressed my palm to my rapidly beating heart. *Oh, be still, my fluttering heart!*

I felt tears burn my eyes. "No one has ever sent me flowers before," I told them. And these were no leftovers with wilted petals. They were just buds, waiting to open up and blossom.

"No one has ever sent me flowers either," Renée said.

Dumbfounded, I stared at her. "Surely Jean-Claude has sent you flowers?"

She shrugged casually. *"Non."*

"He's given you boxes of chocolate, though, right?" I inquired.

She gave her head a quick shake. *"Non."*

I felt like I was in the middle of some bad joke. "He recites poetry to you."

Laughter bubbled out of her then. "Jean-Claude? Poetry? *Non. Non. Non.* He would never read a poem to me."

My legs felt weak. I dropped down on a stool at the counter. "I don't understand. You said he was romantic."

"He is. *Très* romantic," she assured me.

"I'm completely lost here," I confessed. "How can he be romantic when he doesn't do anything special for you?"

She looked taken aback. "What are you talking about? He is romantic because he knows me. He knows when I am sad without me telling him, and he tries to make me happy. When I am not sad, he tries to make me happier. When I am with him, my smile is bigger and my joy is greater. With him, I am complete."

"But he must do something?" I prodded. "Something special."

She shook her head. "He is just who he is. The one I love."

★   ★   ★

By early evening, as I began to prepare for my date, I was still swirling Renée's startling declarations about Jean-Claude through my mind.

I felt sorta betrayed. She'd repeatedly told me that Jean-Claude was romantic . . . and now she'd revealed that he didn't do romantic things. No flowers, no candy, and no poetry.

In essence, he was simply . . . *there*.

I thought about the times I'd seen them together. Jean-Claude always stayed close to Renée, holding her hand or putting an arm around her. At the dance club he'd danced every dance with her. They'd laughed and talked . . . and kissed.

They had looked so . . . well, in love.

She had told me repeatedly that Jean-Claude was a romantic guy, and yet in my opinion, he didn't do romantic things. I was so confused.

I glanced at the beautiful bouquet of flowers that Jacques had sent me. Their fragrance filled my bedroom as I got dressed for my date. As I applied my makeup, my gaze kept darting between my face, the flowers, and Alex's sketch. Flowers were definitely romantic. A sketch? In the annals of romantic history, sketches were probably just a footnote.

But I found that my gaze lingered on it more than it did the flowers. Not because it was a portrait of me, but because the lines had been so meticulously drawn.

Jacques arrived exactly five minutes early. Not early enough to interfere with my getting ready, but

142

early enough to hint that he was anxious for this date. I thought of that old joke about the guy always waiting for the girl to get ready. With Todd, I'd been the one always waiting for him to arrive. Yet here was Jacques, early enough to make me feel special.

And ohmygosh, did he look hot! His black hair was kinda long, but it was combed back off his brow. He wore a black blazer over a lilac shirt. In Mustang a guy would die before he'd wear a pastel shade. White was pretty much standard for any shirt that buttoned. I thought of the blue shirt Alex had worn, but then, he really wasn't typical Mustang.

I turned my attention back to Jacques and his dancing blue eyes. He wore black slacks and had a killer smile. Nice and symmetric, both sides curling up evenly. So far, he was scoring perfect threes across the chart.

"Ready?" he asked in a husky voice.

"Wow," I whispered when I got a good look at his car. I felt like Cinderella stepping into the pumpkin turned coach as I climbed into his black Mercedes.

"I borrowed my parents' car," he explained as he started the vehicle.

And we were on our way to what had already begun as the most romantic evening in my life.

The restaurant—La Tour d'Argent—was the ulti-mate in luxury. Jacques had somehow managed to get us a table by the window, and we had a gorgeous, panoramic view. It was so romantic that it took my breath away.

The food was incredibly expensive. It should have made me feel special, but it made me feel a little guilty. Jacques was going out of his way to impress me, and all I could do was think about Alex.

I felt like I was in a library. Everyone spoke in hushed whispers. The ambiance was something I'd never find in Mustang. In the center of our table a tall, tapered candle flickered. At its base was a circle of orchids. We were even drinking wine.

Well, Jacques drank wine. I'd taken one sip and decided to go with hot tea.

"Any idea what Alex is doing tonight?" I asked.

"He took off cycling just before I left," Jacques explained.

"He really cycles a lot," I murmured.

"Every morning and most evenings," Jacques concurred.

"Do you cycle?" I asked.

"*Oui*. I can barely keep up with Alex, though," he confessed.

"He is amazing," I enthused.

He leaned forward, his blue eyes darkening. "You think so?"

"Absolutely."

Jacques leaned back. "Do you like the restaurant?"

I nodded enthusiastically. "It's gorgeous."

A corner of his mouth quirked up. "Alex thought you would like it."

"He did?" I inquired.

"*Oui*. He thought it would be a romantic place, and he said you liked romance," Jacques explained.

Somehow the restaurant lost some of its romantic edge. Knowing Jacques had brought me here at Alex's suggestion made it seem less special. Maybe I was selfish, but I wanted my date to take me someplace that he thought I'd like. That was so unfair to Jacques, who was paying a fortune for our meal.

I touched his hand. "I also want to thank you for the flowers."

He blinked, looking somewhat dumbfounded. "The flowers?"

"The roses you sent this afternoon," I reminded him.

"Ah." He nodded thoughtfully. "The roses. Of course. I forgot about them. They were nothing."

"Hardly nothing," I told him. "They were lovely."

"I am glad you were pleased."

I tapped my fingers on the table. We'd discussed the restaurant, the flowers, cycling. . . . This was the most romantic night of my life. Renée's words kept swirling through my mind.

And as nice as Jacques was, as attentive as he was, I couldn't help but wonder what Alex was doing this evening. Who had he gone on a date with?

I stood outside the door to Renée's house.

"I had a wonderful time, Jacques," I told him. And I had. Or at least I should have. He'd done everything right. Everything romantic.

145

"I'm glad," he whispered just before he leaned down and kissed me.

It was a sweet kiss. Much better than Todd's kisses, not quite as heavenly as Alex's. It was simply . . . pleasant.

He drew back and gave me a small smile. "*Bonsoir,* Dana."

"*Bonsoir.*" I went inside the house.

Renée pounced on me. She'd been sitting on the couch with Jean-Claude, watching a movie. "So, how did it go?

"It was probably the most romantic evening I've ever had," I acknowledged. After dinner we'd walked along the Seine, hand in hand.

I turned and started up the stairs, wondering why the most romantic evening of my life had felt so terribly wrong.

Eighteen

Alex

WORRYING ABOUT STUFF was starting to get wearisome. In particular, worrying about Dana. Lying on my bed, I watched her pink cap go round and round as I twirled it on the end of my finger.

Earlier in the evening, right after I'd walked past the bathroom and seen Jacques shaving for his big date, I'd thrown on my cycling clothes and hit the road.

Fast and hard. I'd taken corners like a maniac. Pushed myself up hills and soared down at breakneck speeds. Stupid. Dangerous.

But I was trying to escape the image of them in the fancy restaurant Jacques had agreed to take her to—with me splitting half the cost of the meal.

But escape was impossible. I'd returned home exhausted, too tired to hold the images at bay.

I could envision the candlelight flickering over Dana's face, highlighting her hair, reflecting in her green eyes. I could see her sweet smile grow warm as Jacques charmed her with French and courtly grace.

As an all-American boy, the image should have made me gag, but I knew how much all those things meant to Dana, and I wanted her to have them. Even if I wasn't the one giving them to her.

I heard footsteps in the hallway. Jacques's footsteps. I glanced at my watch. It was only nine o'clock. He should have kept her out until midnight.

I bolted off the bed and rushed into the hallway. Jacques stopped dead in his tracks as I advanced on him. "What are you doing home so early?" I demanded.

He shrugged. "The date ended."

"What do you mean, it ended?" I insisted.

"We did all there was to do," he explained.

By nine o'clock? I was baffled and disappointed. "So, how did it go?"

Jacques sighed heavily. "It went well, I think. It would have been smoother if you'd told me that you sent her flowers."

"What do you mean?" I asked.

"She thanked me for the flowers, but it took me a minute to figure out what she was talking about," he explained.

"Oh, sorry. It didn't occur to me that you'd discuss the flowers. Guess it should have. How about everything else?" I asked.

"I did everything you told me to do. Dinner at Tour d'Argent, a stroll along the Seine, a kiss good night," he murmured.

"I didn't say anything about kissing her," I retorted.

He quirked a brow. "How can you have romance with no passion?"

Why did I have the feeling that he was baiting me? I took a deep breath, trying to calm myself. He was right. Dana would have expected a romantic kiss. I just didn't want to think about Jacques kissing Dana—or her kissing him. "Then she had a good time," I admitted.

Jacques shook his head slowly. "I don't think so."

I went completely postal. "What do you mean, you don't think so? Dana wants to date a romantic French guy. You're perfect for her—if you did everything that I told you to. So why didn't she have a good time?"

Jacques gave me a sympathetic smile. "Because, *mon frère,* I'm not the one she loves."

I heard a clock downstairs chime midnight as I lay in bed, thinking about Dana. Earlier, Jacques had explained that I'd been the main topic of conversation during his date with Dana. Dana talked about me so much that Jacques had felt like I was sitting at the table with them. As much as I cared for Dana, I knew that I was totally wrong for her.

I wasn't French, but more than that, I came

149

from a broken family. And so did she. Neither of us had an example of a lasting relationship to build on.

I'd thought that I did. Sure, my parents argued, sometimes my mom cried . . . but they had always managed to work things out. Or so I'd thought.

I remembered Dana telling me how much happier her parents were now. When I'd spoken with my dad, after he'd gotten over the shock of hearing from me, he'd sounded relaxed, more relaxed than I'd ever heard.

I thought about the way it had felt to have Dana rub my back while I talked with my dad. It seemed so natural to have her there.

But no matter how much I cared for her, I knew Jacques was wrong. She didn't love me. She couldn't possibly. We hadn't been dating. We weren't boyfriend and girlfriend. We were just friends. That's all we could be.

She wanted romance, and I was the least romantic guy I knew.

But within my chest, near my heart, there was a little spark of hope. What if I *was* what she truly wanted?

Much to my surprise, Dana called me the next morning.

"Hey," she said sounding slightly uncomfortable.

"Hey, back," I replied. I stared out the window. The sun was shining brightly. Jacques and I had planned to cycle a hundred miles as soon as we finished breakfast.

"I have a huge favor to ask," she announced softly.

I could hear the nervousness in her voice. I figured she wanted another date with romantic Jacques and the sooner, the better. Only she didn't know how to arrange it.

"So ask," I prompted when she didn't continue.

She cleared her throat. "Um . . . well, I was wondering if you'd mind spending the day with me. Today."

"Spend the day with you?" I repeated, clearly stunned.

She released a nervous laugh. "This is so awkward. Do you remember Robin Carter?"

I blinked. "From Mustang?"

"Yes. Well, she's one of my best friends, and she's spending the year as a student in London. Today she's coming to Paris, and she's bringing Kit."

"Who's Kit?" I interrupted.

"He started out as her host brother, but now he's her boyfriend. Anyway, they're going to take the Channel Tunnel rail service. It's only a three-hour trip, so they'll be here around ten o'clock. And we'll spend the day sight-seeing."

"And you want me there because . . ." I let my voice trail off. I wanted her to say that she wanted me there because I meant something to her. After all, I had a life, plans for the day too. You didn't just drop everything because some girl who meant nothing to you called. The problem was, though, that Dana meant something to me. Much more than I'd ever expected her to. More than I wanted her to.

"So Kit won't feel like a third wheel. It's awkward when you have an odd number in a group," she explained.

Not as awkward as realizing that you wanted to be as important to someone as she was to you.

"Why didn't you ask Jacques?" I inquired.

She gasped. "I couldn't ask him. It's not like this is a date or anything, and I wouldn't want him to get the wrong impression."

My pounding heart settled down. It wasn't a date. "What impression?"

"That I cared for him more than I do," she answered.

"Didn't you have a good time last night?" I asked.

She hesitated. "It was really nice. He was really nice. He did so many romantic things."

"So you had your Paris romance," I announced, glad I'd given her what she wanted.

She sighed. "Not really."

"What do you mean, 'not really'? You said he was romantic," I reminded her.

"No, I said he did romantic things. I can't explain it, Alex. It should have been the most romantic night of my life, but it wasn't romantic." Her voice trailed off. She not only sounded disappointed, but sad.

"How could it not be romantic?" I demanded. "It cost me—" I snapped my mouth closed. She didn't need to know how much I'd spent on her romantic evening.

"What cost you?" she asked.

"Nothing," I replied, annoyed with Jacques. More annoyed with myself. "I'll spend the day with you."

"It doesn't sound like you want to." I heard the caution in her voice.

"I do. Honestly. Just tell me where and when." I could cycle anytime. Dana was more important.

"The Notre Dame cathedral at eleven."

"Great. We can take the Metro together. I'll drop by your house about ten-thirty."

I hung up and stared at the phone. Girls were completely illogical. She'd admitted that Jacques had done romantic things. So how in the world could the night have not been romantic?

Jacques's words echoed in my mind. "Because, *mon frère,* I'm not the one she loves."

And I wondered why it was that when either Dana or I needed something, we turned to each other. And more, I wondered why it was that I so quickly changed my plans to accommodate Dana.

And why I always felt glad that I had.

Private Internet Chat Room

Dana: Jeez, Carrie, I wish you could be here. The day just won't be the same without you.

Carrie: I wish I could be there too, but Paris is quite a ways from Rome.

Dana: How are things going with Antonio?

Carrie: Well, he found out that I'm an American, and basically he hates me.

Dana: Bummer.

Carrie: I deserved it. He had this unflattering impression of what American girls were like. I wanted to prove him wrong. Instead I showed him exactly how right he was. I deceived him, Dana.

Dana: I'm really sorry, Carrie.

Carrie: I need to go. Give Robin a hug for me.

Dana: Okay. Take care.

I sat there, staring at the empty chat room for the longest time. We'd all had such glorious plans for our year abroad. So far, only Robin had achieved her dream—and it wasn't her original dream.

I wished I wasn't finding it so difficult to identify what my dream was. I'd lost it somewhere between a kiss on the hilltop and what should have been the most romantic night of my life. And now I didn't know how to recapture the dream.

Nineteen

Dana

"DID YOU SEE Disney's *The Hunchback of Notre Dame*?" Alex asked me.

We were standing at the West Front of what I figured was the most famous cathedral in the world. In answer to his question, I simply arched a brow.

He gave me his lopsided grin. "Stupid question. You probably have it on video," he speculated.

I smiled brightly. "That's right. I own all the animated movies that Disney has released on video."

"You could have your own Disney film festival," he teased.

I shrugged, slightly embarrassed. "Most kids our age wouldn't be interested in animated movies."

"I am," he responded quickly.

And I knew he was. I was constantly amazed to discover how much we had in common. "Maybe when

155

we get home, I'll invite you over to watch them."

"Do that. I'll bring my Pixar collection."

Had I just set us up for a date? No way. I was not dating Alex Turner. Ever. Not here in Paris and certainly not in Mustang. Yet here I was, as always, enjoying his company. I thought about how much more I would have enjoyed that fancy French restaurant if Alex had taken me. The conversation wouldn't have been so stilted or forced. Jacques was nice. He really was, but I'd just never been able to relax.

I shoved my hands into my pockets and turned away from him. "Where's Robin?"

I scanned the sea of faces. So many people were coming to the cathedral today.

And then I saw her. Bouncing along. Her smile bright. She was tallish, with short, blond hair and blue eyes. Kit had blond hair and blue eyes and was also tall.

I remembered how horrified she'd been when we'd arrived at the airport in London and she discovered that her host sister was a host brother. But seeing them strolling toward me, her hand nestled in Kit's, it looked like they were getting along really well now.

I knew the moment she spotted me. Her eyes widened, she shrieked, and she released Kit's hand. She rushed up to me and hugged me tight. "Dana, I'm so glad to see you," she announced loudly with her deep Texas accent.

Laughing, I leaned back. "What happened to

whispering, Robin?" I asked. While I'd had a one-day layover in London, Robin had been trying desperately to keep her loud voice and heavy twang hidden from Kit.

"She took pity on me," Kit explained in a wonderful British accent that reminded me of Hugh Grant. "She finally decided to talk normally."

"Normally?" Robin slipped her arm around Kit's and shook her head. "Can you believe this guy likes my accent?"

"I don't just like it; I adore it," he told Robin.

I couldn't believe how happy they looked. Or how in love. It was incredible and wonderful to see. Robin had really been self-conscious about the way she talked. I was glad to know that to Kit, she was perfect.

Just like Alex. Alex with his love of art, cycling, and dreams to work for Pixar. And his dream to find the perfect French girl. He should be on his quest today, but here he was once again with me.

I felt slightly guilty as I turned to him. "Do you remember Robin?"

He stepped closer to me, and my heart sped up. "Sure do. We had English together last year."

Robin's eyes widened. "Oh, right. Alex."

I introduced him to Kit, and then I didn't know what else to say. I knew Robin was wondering why I'd brought him. Even I wasn't sure. The crazy thing was, I had just wanted to see him.

"You know, if we hurry," Alex announced, "we can

catch the eleven-thirty tour of the towers." He looked at me. "If you're interested in seeing the gargoyles."

"Definitely," I admitted.

"I'll get the tickets." He turned to go.

"I'll go with you," Kit said, and fell into step beside Alex.

As soon as they were out of hearing range, Robin grabbed my arm. "What is Alex Turner Johnson doing here?"

I shrugged. "Just Alex Turner. He dropped the Johnson for France. Too many names. Anyway, I invited him."

"Why?"

A good question. "I just thought it would be more comfortable if . . . we were an even number."

"No third-wheel sort of thing," Robin mused.

"Right." I jumped on that reasoning, had used it myself earlier.

"I didn't remember him being so cute," she murmured. "You seem to have been spending a lot of time with him."

"We're just friends," I told her. "Besides, you know my plan: to be romanced by a French guy."

She slipped her arm through mine. "Yeah, and you knew my plan. To get rid of this horrid Texan accent. You see how well that plan worked out."

"You've got Kit, don't you?" I questioned.

She grinned. "Yeah, I've got him. Just be careful that you don't get Alex."

*　　　*　　　*

158

Alex held my hand all the way up the staircase that led to the north tower. Three hundred and eighty-seven steps. Not that I counted.

But the view from the top made the journey worthwhile. We looked out on a magnificent view of Paris. Alex's hand tightened on mine. "Wow."

I stepped closer to him. "It's incredible, isn't it?"

"You know we really need to go to the top of the Eiffel Tower before we leave Paris," he said quietly.

He'd said it as if we were an item, planning to do things together. We weren't. I glanced over at him. "That's so touristy."

He raised a brow. "And this isn't? Dana, we're tourists. Who knows when we'll get back to Paris?"

"You're right. Maybe we could go today while Robin's here," I suggested.

"Sure."

"Do you have that much time?"

He shrugged. "I have as much time as you need."

That was so typical of Alex. Whatever I needed, he seemed willing to give me.

"Don't forget to let me know how much I owe you for the tickets," I told him.

"Don't be dense. I've been wanting to tour Notre Dame, just didn't want to do it by myself," he explained. "The tickets are on me."

"Hey, guys," Robin whispered loudly. "Come see the gargoyles."

"*Les chimères,*" I corrected her.

She jerked her head around. "What?"

"That's what the French call them," I explained.

She held up a hand. "Look, I don't need to learn French. I'm having a hard enough time learning to speak British."

"What are you talking about?" I asked. "The British speak English."

"Which isn't American. They use the same words, but they mean different things. Trust me, it's another language entirely," she retorted.

"And you're mastering it very well," Kit assured her.

She rolled her eyes. "Yeah, right. But enough about me. Why would someone put something that hideous on a church?" She pointed at the gargoyles.

"I think they're cute," Alex and I said at the same time.

I jerked my gaze to his. He simply shrugged and grinned. "Great minds think alike."

"Right," I murmured. It was scary—how much we thought alike. And how perfect it felt to still be holding hands as we looked at the gargoyles and out over Paris.

"Besides, they're rain spouts," Alex added. "When it rains, the rain pours out their mouths. Supposedly it sounds like they're talking then—'glug, glug, glug.'"

"I don't think I'd want to be up here while it was raining," Robin said.

I thought of standing in the rain with Alex the night he called his dad. I wouldn't mind being up

160

here in the rain with him. Or anywhere in the rain with him. A troubling realization.

I didn't count the steps on the walk down. I figured they hadn't lost any during the time we were at the top of the tower. I did notice the way Robin and Kit kept smiling at each other. Robin looked so incredibly happy and content.

But then, why shouldn't she? Her boyfriend was British. He wasn't from boring Mustang.

I glanced over at Alex. Why couldn't he have been French?

Twenty

Alex

THE CATHEDRAL OF Notre Dame was incredible, with flying buttresses, stained-glass windows, incredible arches, and magnificent statues. I could have spent the whole day here. With Dana.

It was really funny. The way we oohed and aahed over the same things. We looked at everything through the eyes of an artist. We appreciated everything with the same intensity.

I couldn't imagine touring a Gothic cathedral with anyone else.

I also realized that if Dana hadn't brought me along, she would have been the third wheel—not Kit. He was majorly absorbed with Robin. And she with him.

I could tell that Dana was a little bummed by that. After all, she'd been friends with Robin for a long time, and I figured she'd hoped for some serious girl talk while Robin was here.

It was midafternoon before we finished our tour of the cathedral. We decided to head toward the Eiffel Tower. After we ate at a café along the way, we'd ride the elevator all the way to the top. A total day of being tourists.

On our way to the métro that would get us to the tower in about ten minutes, we passed street vendors and flower carts. I decided to buy Dana some flowers to cheer her up a little. She wasn't frowning or anything, but I knew that today wasn't all that she'd hoped it would be.

I tugged on her hand. "Come on, let me get you a flower."

She chuckled. "*A* flower? As in *one?* Solitary? Single?"

"Sure, you don't want to have to carry a dozen around all day," I explained. Besides, with one flower, I didn't figure I could be accused of being romantic or coming on to her. One flower was harmless.

The vendor's cart had a whole range of flowers: tulips, carnations, roses, and a slew of others that I didn't know the name for.

She looked over the blossoms. "Hmmm. One flower. Let me see. I like roses."

"Yeah, but I sent you a dozen yesterday. Seems like you'd want some variety." I cursed under my breath as it hit me what I'd confessed. I spoke quickly, trying to cover my blunder. "Roses are fine. What color?"

She snatched her hand out of mine. It was the first time we weren't touching in almost four hours. Strange how much I suddenly missed that loss of contact. She planted her hands on her hips. "You sent the roses?"

I shook my head. "I don't know what I was thinking. I meant to say that Jacques sent you roses." I quirked a brow, trying to look innocent. "Didn't he?"

She nodded thoughtfully, but she looked troubled. "Interesting that when the topic came up last night, he didn't remember sending them. Why is that, do you think?" she asked.

"The guy did so much to be romantic that sending the roses probably just slipped his mind," I lied, hoping she'd drop the subject. I didn't want to ruin whatever fond memories she had of her date with Jacques, even though they didn't seem to be many.

"A pink carnation," she said softly.

"The florist sent only a pink carnation?" I demanded. Those flowers had cost me a fortune.

She tilted her head slightly, still studying me. "No, I'll take a pink carnation now."

Relief swamped me. "Oh, right." I jerked one out of the cart, paid the vendor, and handed it to her.

I watched her sniff at it, all the while her eyes never leaving mine. I wished I knew what she was thinking. Hoped she thought Jacques had sent the flowers. How could I be so careless?

"Dana, look what Kit bought me," Robin announced.

Dana turned around. Robin was holding about two dozen flowers, all varieties, various colors. And Dana held one scraggly-looking carnation.

"Aren't they gorgeous?" Robin crooned. "Isn't Kit just the sweetest?"

Dana smiled. "He's the sweetest."

And I felt like a complete loser. Robin took Kit's hand, and they started walking away. I touched Dana's shoulder. She glanced back at me.

I jerked my thumb toward the flower cart. "You want some more? Giving you just one was so stupid and cheap. Pick out some others."

She shook her head slowly and looked at the flower. "This one's perfect." Then she lifted her gaze to me. "Thanks, Alex."

She reached up and kissed my cheek. Then she took my hand. "Let's go eat."

I fell into step beside her, and the most insane thought flashed through my mind. Why couldn't I have been French?

Twenty-one

Dana

ALEX GUIDED US toward a cozy little café with outdoor seating. I don't know why, but it just seemed when in Paris, I should eat outside beneath the umbrella.

Robin shrieked when she saw the menu—all in French.

I laughed.

"How am I gonna know what to order?" she asked. "I was hoping for bubble and squeak or toad in the hole."

I stared at her. "What?"

She tilted up her nose. "See? I told you it wasn't easy to understand British."

"You eat those things?" I asked.

She nodded. "Every chance I get. So what should we eat here?"

I glanced over at Alex. He blushed. "I can translate only about half the menu," he offered.

"That should be good enough," Kit said. "I fancy some sort of sandwich."

Alex began to translate, and by the time the waiter came over, we'd decided on four *croque monsieurs*—these really yummy ham and cheese sandwiches I couldn't get enough of. "We are really daredevils," I murmured when the waitress walked away.

"Hey, we crossed the Atlantic," Robin reminded me. "That was pretty daring."

"Yes," I had to admit. "It was."

The waiter brought over our drinks. Robin stared at the glasses and the pitcher.

"What is all this?" she asked.

"The closest thing I've found to lemonade," I explained. "They give you fresh lemon juice, and you mix it with water and sugar syrup."

Robin nodded. "Interesting."

We all mixed up a round, and Robin nodded again. "Not bad." She leaned forward. "You know, when I filled out my application for this program, I expected there to be some cultural differences, but I didn't realize how subtle some of them would be or how many."

I smiled warmly. "Me either."

"What have you found to be the hardest thing to do over here, Alex?" she prodded.

He glanced at me. The right side of his mouth tipped up, and for some reason, my heart played a

167

tap dance along my ribs. His brown eyes twinkled. "Take off my shirt in class."

"What?" Robin asked.

"Our sketching class," I explained. "The guys had to remove their shirts so we could sketch . . . the body."

"Whoa. And I thought getting up in front of the class and revealing my goals for the year was hard," Robin told us.

"Did you have to remove your shirt?" Kit asked me.

I felt my face turn hot as I nodded.

"But she got to wear a bathing suit underneath," Alex muttered.

"No fair!" Kit exclaimed.

"That's what I said," Alex chimed in.

Thankfully, our sandwiches arrived and everyone was too busy stuffing their faces to talk much. My gaze continued to drift between the carnation and Alex. And the intense way that he studied the people at the table.

And I knew, knew in my heart that he was going to sketch this moment.

When we finished eating, we headed for the Eiffel Tower. As we got close, Alex asked Kit to run ahead with him.

"It *is* getting late," Kit said as he glanced at his watch. "I suppose we should go check on the line to the lift."

"The lift?" Alex asked.

"The elevator," Robin said. "We'll wait for you over there." She pointed to a spot under the tower.

"Gotcha," Alex said. He leaned toward me and

whispered, "We'll take our time so you can visit with Robin."

Then he and Kit went in search of the elevator, and I had what I'd wanted for so long—some time alone with Robin that would span more than a couple of minutes. And Alex had somehow known that's what I wanted, and he'd made an excuse to get himself and Kit out of the way.

"I don't remember Alex being so nice," Robin told me. I heard the bafflement in her voice.

I twirled my solitary carnation. "I've got a problem, Robin."

Her brow creased. "What?"

"I think I love him," I blurted out.

"And that's a problem because?" she inquired.

"He doesn't want a relationship. He wants a French girl. Someone who speaks only a little English. Someone with willing lips." I spat out the last part. It still irked me that he was looking for that.

"Did he tell you that?" she asked as a bunch of French schoolchildren paraded by.

"Yes," I admitted sulkily. "When I told him that I wanted a French guy."

"You told him that?"

I nodded. "Like I told you in the chat room, he set me up with his host brother. I think he may have even paid for some of the date. And he is definitely the one who sent me the flowers."

"You're kidding?"

I shook my head. It was crazy. I didn't know

169

whether to be happy or sad. Here was this guy doing all these things for me, and he wasn't my boyfriend. But suddenly I wanted him to be. Even if he wasn't French.

"Dana, he obviously likes you," Robin said quietly.

I snapped my gaze to hers. "As a friend."

"I think more than that," she told me.

I heard familiar English-speaking voices. First Alex's, then Kit's. So much for taking their time. I really needed Robin's advice on what to do.

But there wasn't time to ask her any more questions. The guys came over, and Kit looked really bummed.

"It's a two-hour wait to get to the top," he announced. "I'm terribly sorry, Robin, but we're going to have to head back home before that."

She shrugged. "That's okay. Maybe we can come back."

"I wish you would," I told her. I felt tears sting my eyes. It was always so hard to say good-bye to my friends.

She gave me a hug, and I hugged her back—tightly.

"Romance is in the air," she whispered.

For her, maybe. Not for me. All my dreams for this year were crumbling.

We broke apart. She cradled her bouquet of flowers and slipped her hand into Kit's. "Cheerio," she called out with a British accent.

"Au revoir!" I called back as she and Kit started walking away.

I turned to Alex. "Thanks for coming."

"It was fun." He shoved his hands into the pockets of his jeans. "So, did you still want to go to the top?"

I grimaced. "It's a two-hour wait."

"Yeah, but we aren't going anywhere. Unless you've got a hot date," he remarked.

I laughed. "No. How about you?"

He gave me that lopsided grin. "Nope." Then he took my hand. "Let's be tourists a little longer."

We waited in line for a little over two hours, and we talked the entire time. About everything. Home. Mustang. School. Paris. Dreams.

And we held hands.

Finally our turn came to climb into the double-decker yellow elevator and ride to the top of the tower. My hand tightened around Alex's as we began the ascent. Riding up the tower was not a good idea if you were afraid of heights. The third level, which houses the viewing gallery, was 899 feet above the ground.

That's a lot of feet, I thought as everything below us kept getting smaller and smaller and smaller.

When we reached the top, my heart was pounding a mile a minute. I glanced over at Alex. He seemed okay with the height. "We are really high up," I said inanely.

"Be glad it's not a hot day," he suggested. "On hot days the tower is six inches higher due to the metal expanding."

"This is quite high enough, thank you," I said as we stepped onto the platform.

And my breath nearly left my body. The sun was setting, painting a golden glow over Paris. We walked to the railing and simply stood. My back to his chest, his arms around me.

In silence. With no need to say anything.

We watched the sun disappear beyond the horizon and knew it would be another seven hours before our families watched it disappear. In a tapestry of colors the sky faded into black. And one by one the stars came out.

I sighed deeply. "That is so beautiful."

"Just like you," he said quietly.

I turned to face him. He kept his arms around me. I studied his face in the shadows of the night. "You're going to sketch a picture of me and Robin at the café, aren't you?" I asked.

"Probably."

I took a deep breath. "Alex, why didn't you turn in your sketch of the tower that you did that day on the hilltop?"

"Because I didn't draw the tower. I drew you."

"I can't believe you did that when you had all of Paris—"

"Dana, I want dibs on you when we get home," he blurted out.

Stunned, I stared at him. "What? Dibs?" How unromantic was that? "Like calling for the window seat on an airplane?"

He shook his head briskly. "No, nothing like that. It didn't come out right. I just mean that after this year is up and we get back to Mustang, I want to date you."

"You want to date me?" I repeated.

"Yes. You're driving me crazy. I think about you all the time. You're not what I want. Or at least, not what I thought I wanted." He plowed a hand roughly through his hair. "Look, I *know* I'm not what you're looking for right now. I'm not French. I'm not a romantic guy. But I thought maybe once this year was over, since whatever French guy you hook up with won't be in Mustang, that maybe you'd consider dating me."

I was floored and didn't know what to say to his crazy proposition. "You're going to wait a year to date me," I said tentatively.

"Yeah, I understand your dream, Dana. Paris. Romance. There's probably no other time in your life when you can have all that you'll have this year. That's why I set you up with Jacques, tried to make sure he did everything romantic. I want you to have the romance you're looking for," he explained. He released his hold on me and stepped back.

"I'd just like to know that you'd consider going out with me when we get home," he said.

I nodded, still unable to believe what he'd said. "A whole year," I reiterated.

"I'm not saying it'll be easy for me, watching some French guy romance you." I watched him swallow. "But I want you to have your dream."

I felt tears burn the backs of my eyes. "Are you still going to look for your French dream girl?"

He shook his head. "I was miserable with Monique. I wanted a temporary relationship with a French girl, someone who would make me forget about my parents' divorce. The only time it doesn't hurt is when I'm with you."

I couldn't believe this. I sounded like an echo as I asked again, "And you're going to wait a year to be with me?"

He nodded solemnly. "I understand your dream, Dana. I want you to have it. I'd just like a little spark of hope that once you've realized your dream . . . you might make some time for me."

My chest ached with all he was willing to give up for me. "I can't do that, Alex."

He gave me a sad smile. "That's okay. I understand. A year is a long time."

"Exactly. And I don't want to wait that long to be with you," I said quietly.

His eyes widened. "What?"

I took a step closer to him. "You're the most romantic guy I know."

"Hardly," he mumbled.

I looked at the carnation. He grimaced. "I should have bought you more."

I shook my head. "No, you shouldn't have. Don't you see? That's the point. I thought I knew what romance was, but I was wrong. It's not flowers, or poetry, or chocolate. It's someone you can talk with and feel comfortable around. With Jacques you tried to give me what I wanted. And now you're trying to step back so I can have my dream. When all I really want . . . is you."

"You want me?" he rasped. "Now?"

I smiled tenderly. "Now. Tomorrow. The day after that."

He slipped his arms around me and drew me close against him. "Dana, I don't want you to give up your dream."

"Alex, don't you get it? You're my dream."

The corner of his mouth lifted. "I am?"

Smiling warmly, I nodded. "Yeah, you are."

He lowered his head and pressed his lips to mine, so warm and sweet. I slid my arms around his neck. He deepened the kiss in that slow, lazy way of his. No hurry. No rush. Just heat, passion . . . and romance.

Because here I was at the top of the Eiffel Tower, a star-filled night above me, the dazzling lights of the city below me, and the willing lips of the guy I loved playing gently over mine.

It was strange how the realization that I loved Alex just wove itself into my mind. So easily. As if it was something my heart had always known.

Alex rained kisses along my cheek until he reached my ear. He whispered huskily, *"Je t'aime."*

I love you.

My heart melted.

"I love you too," I said softly.

He returned his lips to mine, and I thought this mo-ment was the most romantic thing I'd ever experienced.

And the best part was . . . Alex would be there when my year in Paris came to an end.

Do you ever wonder about falling in love? About members of the opposite sex? Do you need a little friendly advice but have no one to turn to? Well, that's where we come in . . . Jenny and Jake. Send us those questions you're dying to ask, and we'll give you the straight scoop on life and love.

DEAR JAKE

Q: *I used to live next door to my boyfriend, but my family moved last month. Now some girl my age moved into my old house. According to my friends, she's flirting with my boyfriend all the time. What if they hook up? What am I supposed to do about it five towns away?*

MK, New Paltz, NY

A: How about trust your boyfriend? Who says they're going to hook up? And talking to your next-door neighbor and flirting can often look like the same thing to watchful friends. Give the guy the benefit of the doubt. If you're worried to the point of total frustration, why not tell your boyfriend how you feel? You could let him know that you trust him but that you're feeling a little insecure about being so far away and just need some reassurance that the two of you are solid.

Q: *My boyfriend just told me he might want us to break up because he still has feelings for his ex-girlfriend. I'm totally devastated! I don't want to lose him, but no way am I sharing him. How can I make sure he doesn't go back to her?*

AT, Biloxi, MS

A: My heart goes out to you—this is a tough situation to be in. My best advice is for you to let your boyfriend know that you want to be with him and that you hope the two of you will stay together, and then to sit tight. He probably could use some time and space to think; he might even need to see his ex-girlfriend in order to sort out his feelings. One of the toughest things about love is that you can't control how the other person feels. I have my fingers crossed for you.

DEAR JENNY

Q: *I'm madly in love with a counselor at my sleep-away camp. I'm fourteen, and he's seventeen. He says we're not allowed to date—camp policy. I say we would date if we were* *at the same school, so what's the difference? Can you write something that I can show him to change his mind? Thanks, Jenny.*

PO, Winston-Salem, NC

A: Sorry, but no can do. Camp policy is camp policy, and your crush is right to tell you that the two of you cannot be, at least while you're a camper and he's a counselor. He could get in a lot of trouble if he dated you, and so could you. My advice to you is to respect his wishes. I know it's not easy to like someone you can't have, but maybe another guy will catch your eye. . . .

Q: *I'm a sixteen-year-old guy, and I'm dying to know one thing about girls. Why do they tell each other about everything that happens in their lives, including their relationships? My girlfriend tells her friends everything I do and say. I hate that. How can I get her to stop?*

SG, Akron, OH

A: Good luck! Girls tell each other everything because they can. Girls listen, offer advice, and can discuss a subject to death for hours and hours and pick up the same conversation the next morning. It's definitely a girl thing. But you do have a right to be upset.